T0095029

Harvest of
Two Hundred Suns

Harvest of
Two Hundred Suns

Prologue by
Samuel Ruiz García

Translated by
Montserrat Bueno Espinosa de Los Monteros de Aceves

Maus

Copyright © 2010, 2012 by Maus.

Library of Congress Control Number: 2012911895
ISBN: Softcover   978-1-4633-2980-8
                Ebook   978-1-4633-2979-2

All rights reserved. No part of this book may be reproduced or
transmitted in any form or by any means, electronic or mechanical,
including photocopying, recording, or by any information storage
and retrieval system, without permission in writing from the copyright
owner.

This is a work of fiction. All of the characters, names, incidents,
organizations, and dialogue in this novel are either the products of
the author's imagination or are used fictitiously.

This book was printed in the United States of America.

To order additional copies of this book, please contact:
Palibrio
1663 Liberty Drive
Suite 200
Bloomington, IN 47403
Tel: 877.407.5847
Fax: +1.812.355.1576
orders@palibrio.com
408069

To Chirri, Neni, Carmela and the Doctor
because without them
I would never have been able to meet
the Jors, Juan Sa, Eréndira or Montse.

When ladinos pray they ask
for miracles.
When the indigenous pray
they ask for justice.

Los Peligros del Alma
Calixta Güiteras Holmes

A very important acknowledgment

This English edition would not have existed if it had not been for Dr. William Thomas Whitney jr. from the State of Maine, U.S.A. who found the book and translated it on his own, only to give it to me in the most disinterested manner possible. After five years of effort, he and Priscilla Doel of Colby College generously let me work on their personal translation without any hesitation, thereby letting me get it done in very little time in order to introduce it to the English speaking population. They acted in true commitment with social justice by offering it to the reader as soon as could be and to the people this book stands for. As the reader can see, I am very much in debt to both of them for all their effort but even more for their encouragement and friendship, which I expect, will last forever. The reader who might enjoy this little book must be more grateful still, since it might not ever have been published in English if it had not been for Dr. William T. Whitney jr. and his

Spanish consultant Priscilla Doel. To both of them, my most sincere apologies for all my stubbornness and my deepest gratitude forever for they have proven two things I had always suspected about life; first, that friends are much more important than money and second, that life has surprises installed for all of us if we just have the patience to wait for them.

May I also add a grateful thank you to Eloisa Bueno and Roger Cudney who carefully helped me edit this translation and slowly make it as exact as possible. For all their time and care, may they share a little space in this piece of work.

I admit that the characters that appear in this story have no identifiable faces in the real world. They are not, however, spirits devoid of flesh. They embody a multitude of faces, with the exception of two of them:

Tom, whom I met with his hair bleached by the sun and was named in honor of Saint Thomas patron of his Tzeltal world.

And Manuel, who told this story, once he found himself well shaved and a permanent resident of San Cristobal de las Casas, Chiapas.

San Cristobal de Las Casas, 1982.
Maus

PROLOGUE

Conquered people, submitted people, are people without history. Their history is that of their conquerors. Their customs acquire no legitimacy through citizenship except, at most, as discordant curiosities, like distorted sounds of the dominant culture.

This is why, subconsciously, we do not think of the indigenous culture of our country as being part of our own cultural self or as the root that gives rise to whatever is most ancient and peculiar to our Mexican being. We continue repeating the lesson that we were induced to believe: the notion that what is indigenous has no value and that it is not they who offered us the privilege of being responsible citizens of the world, but instead we look back toward the conquest, so exalted and unquestioned that it is felt to be the starting point of our history.

Whoever may not be able to get beyond this vision might recall that our own roots derive from the past and that our ancestors who represent different ethnic groups throughout the country, including those of European origin, had their cultures too. They might also remember that those pre-Colombian cultures had their own grandeur and what remains of them serves as glorious testimony. We do not recomend this book to whoever is ashamed of the present that the past has been reduced to.

This work cannot be understood if one chooses to view it as an effort to translate or interpret the indigenous world of Chiapas into the Mexico of today. It is neither an anthropological popularization, nor an exercise in reconstructing the life circumstances of an ethnic population.

This work is not to be taken as, and the autor does not intend it to be, a piece of literatura in search of a prize. Although, as a story passed on from mother to son, it possesses a definite beauty. The book has no intention of being pleasant reading.

This work whether one discovers it or not, is written from the inside, from close empathy with the indigenous people. For that reason, much that may seem exotic or incomprehensible is not translated.

This work arises from the need to shout out, from the depths, the painful circumstances of the exploited Indian, as he and she- they themselves - live it, shout it, and cry for it in their prayers, full of tears and mystical elevation. On that account, its characters are brutally real since they are a condensation derived from thousands of men, women, old people, and children...

This work is then an unadulterated cry of silent protest– as are the indigenous people themselves in Mexico –one that goes on like a lament. It is a prolonged cry, one gagged under political and revolutionary slogans, or behind a marginal religion that denies official citizenship to ethnic people, or concedes it only out of compassion.

This work comes to light at a time when Mayan suffering is under scrutiny in Mexico. It echoes throughout the jungle of Chiapas and resounds in the international conscience like a cry that will not be silenced, neither with guns on one side of the Usumacinta, nor by resettlements on this side of its broad flow.

Unprecedented words of libertarian protest are now being forged out of confrontations and resistance to despotic, passive-aggressive Mestizos who rationalize cheap hand labor on the coffee and sugar plantations and who carry out repression that silences organized demands for the satisfaction of claims. They come too from dismay at screams and senseless quarrels from futile attempts to drown one's pains in alcohol – all for the benefit of the bartender or loan shark. It is being stammered out in various organized forms.

A price is being paid, for their debts and other's also, in the disappearances, the tortured, the imprisoned, and the murdered. But one begins to listen for its resonance and feels it like a palpitation of hope drawing near, distant though it still may be.

Here is a syllable of that word, early in its development. You, I, and others join the chorus and sing along with the author, beloved reader.

Samuel Ruíz García
A Walker Among the Mayan
Bishop of San Cristóbal Las Casas, Chiapas.

CHAPTER ONE

There was no explanation for why Santiago was taking so long. Micaela waited for the sun to rise before going down the road.

"Anita, take care of the children, I won't be long."

Her departure disturbed Anita, who was still in bed. Micaela picked up her rebozo* and took down the crossbar that kept the door closed against the cold, thieves, and all the evils that rob us of our sleep. She was so used to opening the door, that the crossbar from the heart and core of solid oak did not even seem heavy to her. She opened the door and walked over toward the center of the village.

Yesterday there were no tortillas, the day before they had been rationed to two per person.

---

* *rebozo, shawl*

There was nothing in the garden, and there had been no beans since the last full moon, which was about to become round again. The blood from her womb forced Micaela into keeping a precise account of her hunger, another month without Santiago, another without expecting a baby had gone by. That is why she walked that morning feeling the cold upon her skin and in her soul.

"Good morning friend, I was just wondering if you have any news about Santiago."

"Well let me see. When we took off and went down the road on our way to the plantation, we were together. When that fat guy showed up, the one without a shave who showed us that money, Santiago just stared at the bills and I noticed how much he wanted them. That was why the guy put them right in front of our eyes so we could feel the temptation. Then he handed over exactly 100 pesos to each of us, which smelled like toasted corn to me. Santiago probably thought the same thing only he mentioned that they smelled like warm beans but of the ones he had at home so when the man told us we would eat well at the finca, all we remembered were the sour tortillas and the rotten beans we had eaten there before. That's when we warned him that this time we weren't going to put up with cold or hunger. We clearly understood we would get better pay. Bullshit, he gave us five pesos more a day for finishing the job."

Chapter I

Santiago mentioned it before he left home. He knew what he was in for. The first time he went off to the coffee plantation was to get a few pennies together to put up a house for Micaela. He was young then and they were both still virgins, since neither had ever been married. If it had not been that he had lost the harvest this year he would not even have thought of taking the money.

He had done it for Micaela, her children, Anita, her child, her baby still to come, and for his mother who was old and deserved some rest. He did it for them, not for himself, and he had barely taken the money, when he began to regret it. The recruiter knew what Santiago was thinking. That is why he took off right away because he knew Santiago would keep his word, like others of his kind. Those who have never seen a written word must be true to what he or she says, so he couldn't break a promise. The deal was done even though there was no contract between them. He knew he had to go do the job and was forced into a deal he didn't want at all. Santiago had to show up afterwards at the finca. Without signing anything, he was forced to honor his commitment and accept a deal with someone who disregarded his customs and who hated his culture. He went to fulfill his obligation and just had not returned.

"I started the journey back last week. Santiago wanted to stay on to get a few more cents together."

"Did he send me any word; did he send me any reason?"

"No, not a word, he was well, that's why he stayed for a few more days. I had to come back now, because I can't work that much. I'm not that young anymore and the work was too hard. But Santiago is a lot younger than me. No, he didn't even get sick. Who knows what happened to him? I am back now, all worn out, and the pay won't last until the harvest."

Why did Santiago go, if he knew it wouldn't solve anything? Now he would be coming back not just poor, but poor and sick also. That dammed land owner, he showed up like snakes do, when you are messed up anyway. The guy just appeared when they had realized there would not be enough corn at home to finish out the year. It seemed as though he could feel the pulse of anxiety. Back then there had been some hope. At least there was a man around the house and they would have been able to do something together. Now there was nothing left, not strength, nor ideas, nor Santiago.

Micaela said goodbye with great sadness. There was nothing more to say. Her friends understood and did not invite her in, as they usually did, because they knew that they couldn't offer her what she was looking for. Micaela left without a tortilla, coffee, or something that might have warmed her body up. It was no longer a question of rationing out the portions. The food was gone. All they could do was to sell the pig. That way the chickens would be left over in case someone got sick.

She walked straight home, thinking about how to get some money. She had to talk with Me'el to get permission to sell the little creature. She felt the need to consult with someone other than her mother-in-law. She wanted to discuss it with Santiago, because he would have thought it over calmly and then have told her what to do. Only that way would she be sure of not making a mistake. With no one around for support, her need for him, her companion, became stronger.

She sat bluntly in front of the warm fire that Me'el had started. The children were still asleep in the room but began to wake up as they overheard the conversation. They never kept secrets from the children anyway. They were the first to feel cold, hunger, and especially their mother's worries. It just was not possible to deceive them. The two women spoke carefully. Anita listened in. As she was neither Santiago's mother, nor his first woman, she remained quiet.

"We'll sell the piglet," said the grandmother, "What else can we do?"

They were reluctant to even talk about it. Where would they take it? What price would they get? How would they carry it? How much would it cost to go? And what would happen when that money was spent?

Santiago had to come back soon. They could only worry about the day ahead of them. Me'el suggested what was always suggested; go down to Jovel* with what little they had and sell it.

Micaela thought otherwise, "We might try to sell it here. Why spend so much on the trip just to end up having to talk to a bunch of traitors?"

"Don't you think that whoever is able to buy it from you here isn't a sneaky ladino** also? At least there are more buyers there. We can get a better deal."

They caught the little creature. Micaela heard the roosters crowing. It was early morning, slightly dark and the stars were still out. There was barely enough time to leave for the market. They would need money for a ride, because it was too late to get to the market by hiking over the mountains, it was way too late to walk.

Micaela was wondering if her mother-in-law could have any money, she just had to. She always did when it was really needed. Micaela was startled when she got back to the house with the little pig and saw that grandma pulled some coins out of somewhere.

"This is what is left of what my son gave me. We have enough for the trip and we should go today. We have to sell the pig now because we don't know what God may say tomorrow and He might not let me

---

* Jovel, indigenous name for the city of San Cristobal Las Casas, Chiapas
** ladino a person born of indigenous ancestors, not Spanish but no longer a member of the indigenous community, often considered a traitor to the Indians.

help you. It's not going to be easy to take that little pig with our bare hands."

Drivers don't always want to carry live animals and they charge more when they do. The two women knew they could go by foot to Jovel but were concerned about the animal losing weight. They were wondering how much weight it could loose. They couldn't carry him that far either, it is not like carrying a lifeless bundle. A sack doesn't wiggle around. A little sow truely defends itself if it is being taken to the market. They can lose a lot of weight on a journey like that. In fact they can even avoid being taken. There was no other choice but to wait for some truck to pick them up.

Me'el was right. It wasn't a good idea to try to sell it there in Cuxuljá where no one had any money. Whoever kept the animal would have to owe them some and they needed corn badly. They didn't dare dream of eating the pig themselves. What a luxury! They would gobble it up, it would be finished in a moment and they would not even have enough money for some corn. Micaela regained her confidence. She went over the accounts and summed up a period of calmness since Santiago could not take that long in coming back. That removed a little of the heavy load that weighed on her conscience, since she kept close in mind that the little animal was being fattened for Santiago's political commitment and duty with the church. She no longer worried about that since

Santiago would have money when he came back. He would then see what he could offer for the celebration of the Saint. When he arrived, there would be food and at least there would be a pair of strong arms around the house.

Micaela tried to forget what little she knew about the fincas,* and Santiago had never said much. He did say that in order to imagine them, men who take their women along with them are those who don't even have a house to leave them in, because no one would want to see their women that way. Micaela at least had her adobe house with long shingles on the roof. Although it was plain and not made of "real material," it was her house and really quite pretty.

She understood that it was best not to leave home, or at least to leave it as little as possible. Nothing bad happened there and she preferred not to know anything about the fincas.* Santiago, who had been to the worst of them, said they were all alike and all crowded. If you followed your husband there you would only make his situation even worse.

At home, Micaela could do what she wanted, with Me'el's approval, of course. She would never have thought of doing anything that her mother-in-law would not have agreed to anyway. What would her own dead parents say if she did something improper? So she was quite content at home, because she did

---

* finca large plantation either of coffee, cotton, banana or sugar with hard labor conditions.

what she wanted, which always was what everyone else wanted.

Right now, on the way to the truck stop, trotting along with short, steady steps and pulling the little animal, she could hardly think about anything else. She forced herself not to think about the coffee plantations but it was almost impossible, since she did not know if she was doing the right thing. What would Santiago have done in her place? Would he have sold the little pig? Would he have asked for a loan? What would he have done?

The two of them were used to walking for twelve hours at a stretch, and for Micaela, a round trip in a truck seemed restful. Once the animal was sold she would have some money for the way back. She thought about saving the fare and splurging it on a watermelon for the children. Me'el also thought about that. She also preferred to carry the bundles on her back all the way home through the mountains than spend the precious pennies they were going to obtain.

They were on their way to the truck stop on the highway, but the little pig, not used to all this was distracted by every rock along the road. The two women armed themselves with patience and calmly led him along. Micaela pulled from the front and Me'el, stick in hand, walked behind to keep him from going astray.

The grandmother, like Micaela, was quite used to walking all day, and she never saw a truck in her entire childhood. Anyone who left from Oxchuc did so on foot and had to walk for many miles. They took long treks carrying heavy packs secured by straps around their foreheads. Today, for some miraculous reason, she was not carrying anything and would be traveling comfortably in a truck. On the way back she would also be loaded down with the sacks that they were going to buy, that was why she was traveling in order to help with whatever was needed.

It was as cold as it always is in February but walking helped them get warmer. Me'el wanted the soil to warm up also so that it would dry up. Walking on solid earth is much easier than through mud. Me'el went along without stumbling but she knew she was fragile because of her age so she was always afraid of falling. A fall is very dangerous and she knew it. It would have been too much bad luck, almost a trick of the devil, to have to deal with more misfortune now, on top of all of their other problems. You have to watch out for the devil more because of his clever tricks than his outright wickedness, because he butts in and can strike a person down for an entire lifetime. What might look like a street dog may be haunted, aggressive and full of tricks. Thinking about misfortune is like whistling to a cur. Never beckon the devil because he'll come and that's the way evil things are done. The devil plays his tricks and makes you fall so you think you fell by yourself, on your own accord, and it even looks like you fell alone. You don't have to whistle to a cur. He'll appear all by himself just like a street dog aggressive and sly.

What if something happened to her? Who would take care of so many children? They would take care of themselves, like she had done with no mother, no father and no name. The Saints would take care of them. But why worry about that now when what was important was to reach the market on time. At last the two women stopped for a moment in the shade of an oak tree near the crossroads. They waited there for the truck from Ocosingo to pick them up.

They tied up the little animal and sat down to cool off in the shade. Me'el took a lump of cornmeal* out of her knapsack.

There was just a little for the rest of the trip. While they were away the children at home would only have vegetable pear to boil and eat. But children do play and playing makes them forget their hunger plus they wouldn't take long since they were already negotiating the cost of the ride on the truck.

"Please charge me just a little, don Ramon."

"I am going to charge double because of the little pig."

"Sir, just a little bit!"

"It takes up too much space, that's not a good deal, it'll cost you a double rate."

"It's not worth it. I am taking the pig to sell.

---

* *cornmeal or pozol*

"Let's walk," interrupted the old woman. "Forget the truck." Whispered the old lady in her native Tzeltal language.

Micaela wanted to get back home soon. The little ones were all alone, and, besides, traveling with a live animal is not the same as carrying a lifeless sack.

"OK. Get up there then. I'll only charge you one fee, but it's just for you, Micaela."

Don Ramon helped her up. Together they tied the pig to the side rails.

"Why are you selling your pig, Micaela?"

"For money."

"You don't have to do that. You know that you don't have to do that."

"So then, how can I pay a Kaxlan* truck driver his fare?"

Don Ramon didn't dare look straight into her eyes. Ashamed, he got down from the truck and kept on taking fares. Micaela worried that someone might have heard her. She turned around to check out whether anyone was staring, but no one seemed curious. Mel certainly had not heard anything, because she would not have climbed up into the truck. There she was with a smile on her face as always, showing the loss of what once were bright white teeth.

They left at last and the day was just beginning. In two hours they would be in Jovel. The truck railings

---

* Kaxlan disrespectful term for those who are not indigenous meaning people with chicken egg colored skin.

Chapter I

ᒪᒪᒪ

were shaking, as they themselves were, along with the rest of the passengers. Micaela went over the pictures running through her mind. To tie her thoughts together, she rested her head on the rails and let her mind run free.

The images also lead to Santiago. She tried to distract herself, but the feeling that Santiago was suffering was stabbing her heart. The only thing that seemed to bring relief was the thought of him getting close to caress her. She kept thinking about him so that the sensation would keep other worries away. Even though she was familiar with every part of his body, she was unable to visualize it completely. Her memory was betraying her, because the images insisted on fading and she could reproduce only fragments of recollection that kept fading away. She managed to remember the look in his eyes, how prominent his jaws were and how tan and slim he was. The only piece of memory that she managed to focus on loyally was his manly style. He had an easy bearing, proud and gentlemanly. Micaela let her thoughts about Santiago travel with her until the noise of the side rails broke into her mind. The trip was long and soon all memories gave way to the true discomfort of fatigue.

Only one more hill and they would be in San Cristobal. Me'el looked out through the wood slats hemming her in. Her memory played tricks on her. She could remember very little about yesterday, but even so, that hill brought her entire childhood right up to the present.

How many times had they not arrived there walking all together to that precise hill? Only one more mountain and then they would be in Jovel. From the foot of the hillside where she now was each mountain seemed like a temple that had to be climbed one by one to get to Jovel. Me'el saw the spot where the night generally set up the rules and they had to decide where to camp out to keep warm. It was useless to enter Jovel at night. There was nothing in the market and no place to sleep. No one would take them in with bundles or live animals and they had no money for beds. They would have had to sleep on the sidewalk and risk being arrested. So they would spend the night in the woods gathering up a few sticks to warm themselves up with a fire.

Me'el was good at making fires. Since she was a little girl Me'el learned how to place them so as to light up an entire hillside. She would erase her fear that way because evil things come out at night, which is when animals go hunting. They take advantage of the dark and harm whatever is left out unattended. So Me'el was always afraid in the woods and she stuck close to her brother's side. He never knew why she leaned on him that way. He would push her away just to be able to move around better, so she would just stay close touching him slightly with a finger or a toe so as to feel him nearby. Then when her own children did the same thing with her, she never turned them away. She knew they were afraid so she stayed close to them.

They all did the same thing, all but Santiago. Who knows why he was never afraid of the night? Perhaps because he was the eldest, he was always in one piece, even during the first half- hour after midnight, when they stayed absolutely quiet to keep from provoking the spirits. And where could Santiago be now? They would have to ask the fire about him. If he had not arrived when they returned home, that very night she would ask the salt.

For the moment, there was no way to find out. Me'el almost thought she saw him, obediently taking his place at her side along the road. All her past became present as the last tones that the sunrise had left behind faded away. She saw the last hill on the road where so often, as a child, she had slept in the open and where later on she saw her own children feel just as cold.

They were at the curve in the highway where the view opened up over a valley greener than jade. Micaela knew they had arrived in San Cristobal.

They ran into their first enemy as soon as they got down from the truck.

"Well then, where are you taking that little animal?"

"We want to sell it."

"500 pesos here right now, so you don't get all tired out. See. I am just going to help you. I will pay you right here, so that you don't have to go all the way over to the market. It's a long way off.

Come on, take your money so you can head back to your ranch."

She was offering very little, by no means enough to save a few steps to the market.

"We want 1000."

"1000! Who is going to pay you 1000 pesos for that little runt? I want to look at it and see if it has any pus sacks."

"That's not enough, not even enough to pay for the trip."

"What do you mean, it's not enough? What do you want so much money for? That's enough for both of you. You can get more than enough corn for the two of you with that much money. Let's see. Let me look at it to see if it has pus sacks."

Micaela did not understand.

"Look, stubborn Indian! You just don't understand. I am trying to help you. Now take your money and go home. Otherwise you will end up with nothing. Don't even go all the way over to the market. They will just cheat you there and you will have made the trip in vain. Take your money so you see that I really want to help you. If not, when the sanitary inspector comes by, he will take your animal away from you. Here, take it. I'm giving you a lot more than what it's worth."

She tried unsuccessfully to snatch the pig away and put the money in her fist but Me'el had a firm hold of the pig's collar.

ひヱヱ

"Go back to your village where you were born, stubborn thankless wretches!" shouted the half white woman, as her prey slipped out of her hands ending the conversation. Me'el and Micaela got away from her and in short order were at the market.

Micaela did her business there with the little Spanish she knew. Soon she found someone interested in reselling her little pig for more than 100 pesos per every kilogram that it weighed.

"How much do you want for your little pig?"

"A thousand pesos."

"But he is still on the hoof. He has to be killed. How can I pay you so much?"

"Make an offer then. How much would you give?"

"Let me look at it to see if it has any boils."

He took the pig by the snout and looked under the tongue. If he knew anything after so many years of butchering, it was a sick tongue and this one was clean. The little pig was fat and tender, like ones from the ranch usually are. For 1000 pesos it was a gift. He grabbed the pig with a knife in one hand, as if to slit its throat.

"This one is filled with pus sacks." He told Micaela, who looked over so she could see what the man was pointing to but she just couldn't notice anything. She did not understand and in order to persuade her, the butcher called over to someone working in the next booth. The neighbor agreed about the pus sacks even before showing up.

"It's full of pus."

"Now, you see. You better take the 700 pesos I am giving you and get going. Go on, I am giving you a lot of money. Take it, so you can finish your business once and for all and go home. What are you staying around for? You are going to get caught in the rain. Get going and go on home."

"That is not enough." Micaela knew that it couldn't rain. There had been frost in the early morning so it was a splendid day now.

"But your little pig isn't worth any more, why with pus sacks, it's not worth anything and I am paying you well. Look! Here they are seven 100 peso bills. Take them, come on."

The price was set, 1500 pesos, 2000, even 3000 for those who know how to do business, as low as 750 for those who can be cheated. But the other butcher liked the animal. Pigs raised free-range out in the country have almost no fat and this was a tender one. The second butcher, no longer an ally, became a rival and competed making another offer.

"Look, your little pig has boils, but that doesn't bother me. You see I know how to get rid of them. I will give you 800 pesos for your little animal. Here it is, the exact amount, so you can go home happy. It's done. I am giving you good money. It's more than enough for your beans."

Chapter I

He pushed the money into Micaela's hands before she knew what to say. She had never had so much money in her hands.

Micaela looked at it and didn't know how to count it. She went through it without adding it up. She had no other choice but to trust that man and it was hard to have to trust a ladino.

The first thing Me'el wanted was a drink. She asked for it right away.

"Let's go over there to Uncle Chandito's, my child." The poor woman had gone a long while without pox.* It was forbidden, but she smelled it and could always find the hiding place.

"Have a stout, Me'el, for now."

"Beer's too expensive. I want pox, the kind that anyone would make a long journey for, just for a pint."

There was beer everywhere, it was a rich man's business, but Chandito had a good hand for pox. He was patient and he let it settle. Me'el could get drunk with only ten pesos of pox. It took her too long to get dizzy with beer. Micaela bought some and took a drink herself. She was not that interested in it, but she felt good and celebrated the moment.

With spirits revived, they went over to the sacks of beans. Big buyers always get better prices, but they were not big buyers. They had no friends in the market

---

* *pox alcoholic beverage distilled from sugar*

so when they asked for a discount they had to settle for the top price, that offer was a favor. The saleswoman didn't care for a customer who could not even speak Spanish. Micaela handed over the money and took back her change. She went through the bills just so the saleswoman would see her do it for she had no idea how much money was really there. She mounted the sack on her back and steadied it with a strap over her forehead.

After buying a watermelon they needed to buy salt, so they walked over to another stall. They bought a piece of the brick because it was cheaper that way since it didn't contain iodine but Micaela couldn't see the difference. They went over to another stall for corn and it was the same story. The price was fixed, a little more established for them than for others. There would be no bargaining. Micaela helped her mother-in-law lift the load up onto her back and fix it to the harness around her head.

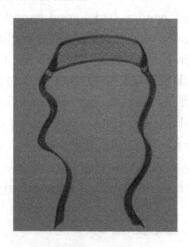

CHAPTER TWO

The purchases were made and the load was now a burden on each of their backs. The two women began their return trip and made their way over to the stairs. There, where the shouts of vendors get confused with the cries of the blind who beg for money at the same time, where the smell of fried fish gets mixed up with the plastic that was just being unwrapped, where the screams of the merchants make a riot, Me'el who knew what it is to have poor vision, put some coins into the hands of the blind man, who was begging for money. She must have done it awkwardly, either that, or she may not have remembered that that stairway is always slippery, because she rolled painfully down the concrete.

Micaela heard her crying out from below. Terrified, she ran down to help her.

"My foot." Me'el cried out again, in tears. But she was more afraid than in pain since the fall was too recent for the pain to be felt with the sharpness that time would give it. She tried to lift herself up but it was impossible. She was used to putting up with a lot of pain and would have walked in spite of it, but her very own foot did not respond and that was her only means of transportation.

She tried to lift herself up, but to no avail. Her ankle, which whimsically did what it wanted, was so swollen it could not be distinguished from the rest of her limb. Micaela did not know what to do for her and not knowing what to do only made her impatient. She almost never visited Jovel and knew no one there. She needed someone who might know how to rub it back to normal. She soon found out where to find a massager from the people who quickly surrounded them.

"Rub it yourself meanwhile. Otherwise it will keep on swelling."

"Wrap it up in something or it will catch a chill."

"Juanita is right over there. Yes, she knows how to rub and set bones. The bonesetter is far away. He is all the way over there by the park."

Taking the crowd's suggestion, they entrusted their sacks to a woman they had never seen before but who offered to look after their things.

"Don't worry. I will look after your beans for you," while they tried to make their way up the stairway toward the tables and benches of the lunch area.

Micaela took Me'el up by supporting her shoulder so that she would not have to put weight on her foot. Steadied by Micaela, Me'el hopped step by step over to the tables. Without even trying to use her foot, she was feeling more and more pain from each bounce. Even thinking about stepping on it brought on shooting pains. Me'el thought that if she could lie down, rest for a while, and make herself comfortable, then the pains might ease up a little.

It was easy to find Juanita. She was at her booth, as always from five o'clock in the morning on. She spoke no Tzeltal but had a friendly smile. Me'el felt reassured when she sensed her gentleness. Friendliness gives great comfort when you are beaten. Even though they had never met before, they immediately had confidence in each other, and Me'el accepted all the suggestions of help that Juanita had to offer.

"Holy Mother, Mary, Josef and Jesus! What happened to you, grandma?"

"It was a fall, a hard blow,"explained the old woman. "I messed myself up. I sure screwed my foot up once and for all," cried Me'el in the little Spanish she knew.

"I need to take care of this, old woman, otherwise it won't get better and it will never get back to what it was."

"It doesn't have to, just as long as it stops hurting. If the pain goes away, I'll see about walking."

"Be patient with yourself. You are going to have to put up with a little pain, so I can fix it for you."

"Do something, for the love of God, do something for me."

Juanita did what she could. She covered the ankle with oil and began to move her fingertips over the swollen flesh. The old woman screamed.

"Dear lady, No! Don't do that. For God's sake, don't do that."

"It hurts, grandma, but you already know that these things hurt."

"This is different. I have never felt so much pain in my life. I can't take any more. Please don't touch me."

The old woman was crying. She covered her lips with her striped rebozo, lips that covered only gums. Juanita did not insist. She felt sorry for the old woman and let go of the foot. She did want to help her but did not know how to. She kept on trying in every way. She got up to roast green leaves on the iron pan. When Me'el saw her doing it, she recognized the plant and prayed.

"Holy Mary, take away the pain."

She knew that that herb took away pain, but she also knew that it couldn't take away this much pain. Instead, she preferred to lift up the jar of pox and press it against her lips. She took a large drink. It was her only remedy.

Sobbing, Me'el clenched her hands tightly tangled up in the twisted strands of her shawl, begging and pleading for the pain to go away. She asked the Saint to help her be cured, that all the evil she might have done be forgiven so that he might be able to help her. Me'el recalled what she was, an old woman who washed beans, who looked after the children, who blew on the cooking fire. She owed nothing to anyone that was dead. Now, unable to even get home, she could only dedicate herself to feel pain.

Juanita brought over the warm leaves and fixed them so as to relieve the shooting pains. The old woman felt relieved when she saw that a strange woman was willing to help her and she thought that she could do something about her foot. Hardships weigh less when they are shared. The presence of the two women who were so concerned about her was consoling.

Once exhausted, she fell asleep. They let her rest and let the leaves cure her. They knew that soon they would be disturbing her again.

"You are going to have to control yourself now. I am going to have to set that bone."

And Juanita proceeded with her work. She took the ankle with her two hands. She fixed the leg upon her knee with one hand and with the other she pressed forcefully where the swelling was. With each movement, the old woman seemed to go insane. She twisted around like a snake. Once and again, Juanita would rub strongly against Me'el's foot but Me'el did not have enough strength to stop her hand. All she could do was feel an unaccountable amount of pain.

Juanita rubbed it for as long as she thought necessary, and Me'el, exhausted, stretched herself out on the bench hoping the pain would go away. She was unable to stop the flow of tears, although she tried. Juanita helped her lie down more comfortably. Micaela asked her to see after Me'el and started to take the bundles with their purchases over to the truck stop. When she returned, she would give Juanita the two pesos she charged for the massage and for the offer of spending all the time they needed on the bench.

"Let her stay here and rest peacefully. I will see that no one wakes her up if she falls asleep. I am not expecting any more customers; all the regular ones have already eaten. There is plenty of room on the bench no one will be using it for a while. You may leave her here."

Micaela went for the bundles to get ready for the trip back. They would never make it to Cuxuljá by walking. She did not want to remind Me'el of her desire to return on foot and keep some of the money for the children. At least they had bought the watermelon. For sure the best part of going back on the truck was that they would be home in four hours instead of eleven or twelve hours of walking. Micaela did not even mention it and looked for the truck. There was no sense in reminding the old woman about it.

Micaela carried over the first bundle and asked how much each ride would cost. She thought that the price for the two bundles they carried was too high, so she went over to another truck. He did her the favor of agreeing to take them, along with the bundles, and he charged less. She ought to have been pleased, but she burst out crying. Paying for the fare took care of any idea of going back with extra money. She was unable to explain to the driver what she felt and stood there sobbing in front of him.

There was still a little bit of money left over, less than she anticipated, but some, and now there was corn. Micaela began to feel reassured. The driver came over to collect the coins from her. His bill was ready. He hid nothing. He was interested both in Micaela and her money.

Micaela had everything paid for and the first sack in the truck. She returned to the market for the other bundle. She wanted Me'el to rest as much as possible. When she came back to check on her, Me'el was deathly pale. Far from improving, she couldn't stand the pain at all. Micaela put Me'el's arm over her shoulder and helped her up. For now, they had to get to the truck and that was very painful.

The driver stood over to one side and didn't offer any help. It was the other people who offered their help in order to get Me'el up. Some of them pulled her from the truck bed while others pushed her from below, taking care not to aggravate her ankle pain. They laid her out on the floor. The driver asked for double the amount, because someone lying down takes up too much space. But everyone protested and Micaela understood why she had never trusted that man.

CHAPTER THREE

It is always a relief to get home. There is a feeling of calmness, as soon as you get in. Micaela unloaded the sacks herself and went back to help her mother-in-law by lending her a shoulder so she could move around. Me'el was truly grateful from the bottom of her heart. She trusted Micaela and appreciated the motherly care she received from her. Getting to the door was not easy so Me'el rested when they finally entered the house.

Anita was not expecting them so soon and from the look on her face they knew that she was not especially happy to have them back. Micaela was uneasy but did not really know why. Who could tell what was going on with Anita? That's the way she was sometimes. She blamed her bad mood and tried to forget it.

Anita realized that something had happened to her mother-in-law. She asked all the details and Micaela told them to her. "She'll get better; her ankle has already been rubbed."

Poor woman, thought Anita. She had never before seen her mother-in-law sick. Me'el was the hardest worker of the three. This was the first time she had ever felt sorry for her. She had so much respect for her ideas and for her few words, which gave her absolute authority, because Me'el knew about death well and relied on the support of many dead people. Anita felt her moral authority in such a way that she always obeyed her. Me'el had already lost four sons and had bidden farewell to her parents and husband, but only for a short while. As a widow and an orphan, Me'el could communicate easily with the dead.

Protected as she was by the Saints and her deceased husband, she maintained the integrity of her soul. Her powerful nahuales* remained at her side, they were not about to leave her. They were settled in firmly, quite used to being close to her. But now she was not so sure she could resist. She had been hurt more than her nature could deal with. She was in danger. Her soul was slowly breaking up into pieces and deteriorating. It was a challenge to her old age. Anita noticed that she wasn't well. She couldn't tell how seriousness the injury was but she had to accept changes in the daily routine. She would have to do Me'el's chores.

Domingo and Mariana were playing under the trees. They had gone out for wood while Maria Rosa and Tom were playing with the yearling lamb, the favorite toy of Micaela's sheperds. The four of

---

* *Nahual; animal spirit that accompanies a human soul living his or her other life in the forest.*

them came in and she asked them about their older brothers. Perhaps they had already come back from the cornfield for their pozol.* She worried about all of her children, the ones on hand now, and the others who were away. She thought she could never pay God back for the children He had given her and especially for not taking anyone away. God knows why He does everything, that's why he gave her two boys first to help her with the smaller ones. Micaela had set corn aside for them in case they came back for it. It would have been a long way for them to come back in vain. She always had it ready for them, because she knew how hard it was to get the soil ready for the seeding. Now she was waiting for them to fill up their packs as always. They had been gone for four days.

Fortunately they already knew how to do the planting. This was the first time they were doing it without Santiago. They had always helped him but had never done the seeding on their own. Most of all, they helped him keep the cornfield clear of weeds because a corn patch needs a lot of care. Micaela intended to go with them the next time they went. It was good to see what the boys were doing and help them a little. In fact, her strong arms were a lot of help. Thank God, she could rely on them. That was exactly what encouraged Santiago and made him go earn a few cents in order to make his children glad.

---

* Pozol, corn boiled and diluted in water, it can be sweetened or salted with chile added to it.

They were good sons, strong, tall and graceful, almost men, and always so happy in the cornfield.

The food was late and Me'el waited patiently to be served. There was enough food now, but that was not a reason for her to over eat. She was hungry and Anita was taking too long. Me'el noticed that she was anxious and uneasy, and not concentrating on her work.

"This girl is sick," she said as she thought out loud relying on her instinct, she had been observing the world for too many years not to notice when someone's appearance was not in order.

"I am fine," said Anita, avoiding any interrogation, and she hurried on to serve the beans.

"Watermelon?" Micaela offered some to her, "It's refreshing just to look at it. Take some to cool yourself down."

Anita was noticeably warm now, more so with the fresh night air coming in through the door cooling things off. With night upon them, the children came in looking for beans and the light from the fire. Right away they swarmed around the bean stew. They were going to be eating beans all week. Sometimes they looked like goats, especially when they cleaned out the orchard, where now not even a single sad peach had been left behind. They ate so much that even the bananas could do them harm. They sometimes picked one bush clean and went to another, from pear to apricot, never tired of eating fruit. Not even indigestion stopped them. But now at the end of winter, the fruit trees looked so sad it seemed like they were in mourning, that's how sad they looked. The hailstorms had not spared a single flower.

"There's going to be some pozol. Don't be impatient."

"We already ate some earlier, we sweetened it up."

"You already had some? Did you eat anything else?"

"Just pozol, and quite a bit, but I'm never too full for some beans."

Micaela looked over to see what the expression on Anita's face revealed but she did not find her as Anita had left the room. She went out after her all set to quiz her.

"Where did you get that corn? Where did you get the money?"

"I did someone else's washing."

"Since when have you been doing other people's laundry? Why didn't we know about this?"

"You know I don't do it often. There was nothing to eat, so I went to the river and from there I went to clean the house of the lady who lives over where the roads cross."

Micaela did not continue her questioning. It was upsetting to try to speak with Anita who wouldn't let her look into her eyes. That was the way Anita was and it was even worse when she was throwing a tantrum.

Chapter III

Me'el tried to make herself comfortable. She moved around a lot and could not find a position that gave her any relief. She made no inquiries about the money that Anita had mysteriously obtained, or about the job they knew nothing about. Me'el did not meddle into other people's business. If there was anything she knew better, it was to keep away from hearsay and gossip. People can say very evil things about others with the slanderous use of their tongues in idle talk. She had a foreboding but kept quiet about it. It would not be the first time Anita brought them a surprise. She knew her well.

Micaela, on the other hand, could not hide her misgivings. As soon as Tom came in, she took advantage and questioned him.

"Did Anita leave this morning."

"She did."

"For a long time?"

"All I know is that she gave us our pozol and asked us to bring in wood. We didn't see her again after that."

Micaela was usually suspicious of anything Anita might do. Curiosity was always stinging her. There was no way she could insist on getting information from her, nor did she have any reason to do so. After all, Anita had not done anything wrong and at least she made sure the children had eaten something. Anita should not be leaving the house without permission and from now on she would have to say where she was going.

Micaela was taking out her own annoyance on Anita. She was tired and it was not the first time she had done that. It was early still. She laid down on the boards she used for a bed. She tried to keep from falling asleep but fell into deep sleep. She struggled against it while she waited for her boys, matched as a pair of oxen, to return from the cornfield.

It took quite a while to get rid of the tension accumulated from the trip, but finally the images that come with the beginning of rest began to flow. With her eyes closed, she watched the marks that life leaves as traces on the soul, go by. They appeared as she got sleepy, first as foggy hazy images and later with intense visions when she was fast asleep.

Ideas passed through her mind like printed images. She allowed them to go by, as she carefully studied them. She remembered her dreams well and was not afraid of them. Dreams do tell us what our heart keeps trying to hide. Micaela tried to keep track of each image as if she were running along behind them. She tried to reach out to them but her efforts were all in vain because exhaustion had its way.

She could have slept until darkness lightened up but woke up because the boys arrived close to midnight. She was so pleased to see Lorenzo and Sebastian that she completely woke up in spite of her fatigue. Micaela sat up to look at them. Her boys were together like a yoke of oxen and the couple talked about the cornfield. Nothing had changed out on the patch of maize and no news was good news. They had begun to chop up the earth and Lorenzo made everything quite clear with his comment.

"There is nothing new! Thank God!"

What she had really worried about had already been done and was finished because the boys had even been able to burn the land without Santiago. Micaela had been worried about the fire taking off. If they were able to do that alone, then they could do everything else. It took extra exertion, of course, because their bodies were still young and could hardly stand the intensity of so much work.

At least Santiago would find the ground ready when he came back. They had made the beds ready for seeding using the only method proven to be useful for centuries, which is a bent back with a hoe in one's hands. They mentioned that the freezing mornings were outright cruel but that the days at least were splendid although a bit too hot and sunny. They were tired out from the heat and at night the cold wind from the north blew on them but they were proud. They wanted Santiago to return and be able to see their work. He would be proud also. That was what they missed most in the cornfield, Santiago's pride and his guidance. They all wanted to have some news about Santiago, hear something, even more now that they were all gathered together around the fire. Two months of his absence had united them. Only he and Manuel were missing but Manuel would be returning from the public boarding school shortly. They would have news about him in a few days. As for Santiago no one knew anything or could know. They all wanted to see him and offer him a warm home that smelled of beans, toasted corn and burning wood.

Seated around the fire and protected by its light, they began to talk. They had to speak about the future with true hope, because the cornfield was being taken care of the way it should be. Now they only depended on chance and it could not betray them. Hugging one another and feeling confident they began their prayers, asking the Saints and the natural forces for their true consideration. They prayed to all the people that were in heaven, to all the wise ones, that lived dead and hid* in the mountains. Calling upon the nobility of all the Saints, they asked that they negotiate good fortune for them before the Almighty, so that justice might be done. Me'el wanted to ask the Saints something that only they could know. Micaela, Anita, and the children joined together in a chorus:

"Me'el, please ask the salt where Santiago is."

Mariana got up right away and brought over the lumps of salt. She always did favors for Me'el and enjoyed helping and talking with her. She would have done the favor of bringing the lumps over in any case,

---

* Dead ancestors are believed to live in the forest and take care of our nahuales.

even if Me'el had not been hurting. Me'el never had to beg for a favor from her little granddaughter, and less so now. Mariana handed over the largest lump of salt that she found.

Me'el took the salt and spoke to it. She asked it to tell the truth. She spoke to the fire and asked it to tell the truth. She spoke to the Saints and asked the same thing of them, to tell the truth and nothing but the truth. She took the lump in her fist, squeezed it, and threw it vigorously into the fire. The fire blazed up and the red lump exploded, scattering fragments in the air.

Many of them flew off to the left, some to the North, and at least a few went off to the East. But unfortunately they saw how a great ball of salt filled out the cosmic picture with a bad omen, flying towards the South. Santiago was alive. That had just been confirmed, but where was he, how was he? Me'el felt better as soon as she saw the blaze throw the ball following the path of the sun. She had expected more salt to fall in the eastern corner, but she was a little relieved. At least it had taken the road leading towards the end of the day without exploding in the darkest part. A lot had gone astray, much of it, alarmingly enough, off to the South, and they could not help being afraid for Santiago.

Something was wrong. Santiago was not completely well. Anxiety began to spread and disrupt the order of the house, which would not be settled until Santiago's arrival. The women no longer slept well. There were many dangers and they reviewed them all. There were only two things left to do, wait for Me'el's dreams that night and wait for Santiago. The fire could not tell where he was but at least they knew he was alive. The salt had told them so.

Silence replaced their joy and interrupted all the attention they were giving to the fire. The children went to their corners. They held onto each other on their straw mattresses. Tom and Domingo climbed onto the boards they used as beds and did not want to come back down. A little scared and unable to hide their fear, they closed their eyes to wait for a new sunrise, but stayed awake, since they went to bed without feeling sleepy and without blankets, covering themselves with one another.

Domingo started to think about his father being away. The night grew long and he was startled by the thought of his own death. He could not sleep. He was even more frightened by the idea of having to live without anyone to look after him by the time he lost his eyesight completely. He calmed down when he thought of Manuel who would help him. They would never leave him on his own, not Manuel nor Tom even though they were younger than him. They would go to school in his place because Domingo never managed to pass the boarding school's entrance exam. A light constantly glimmering in his eyes kept him from learning how to read. He would not get even an inch of his father's land. There would be nothing for him, except that accursed trachoma, an affliction that had affected all of the children but no one knew why it had been so cruel with Domingo. He just never got well, it just never went away, and now he would live under the protection of Manuel who at least would be well educated. He bore Manuel no resentment for taking his place in the boarding school, because with school he would be able to take better care of him. The relief of having an educated brother made up for his sadness. Otherwise, what would become of him?

As Domingo's thoughts wandered he missed Manuel more than ever before. He was sure he could communicate with his brother beyond the mountains. It was not possible that he did not feel the fear that came over them when they saw the salt's response. Domingo believed that his brother was aware of everything. In desperate need of some understanding, he prayed to his brother, begging Manuel to let him be a part of him. He managed to fall asleep knowing that he would be able to count on his help. He thought that the revelations of the fire would reach Manuel even though he was very far away and he would be worrying uselessly since there was nothing he could do. Domingo felt sorry for Manuel, whom he imagined alone and anxious. He felt the workings of fate, that fervor of spirit and body that brought him back to the same question. "Why did papa leave for the finca?" "Why are we so poor? Why have we been poor all life long if we work so much every day? Why do we never stop being poor?"

Of all questions with no answer, Domingo, who was barely eight years old, wanted to answer the most difficult one of all, one that he would ask and leave unanswered so many times in his lifetime. Why were they so poor, even though they all worked all the time and they worked so much everyday? Not a good night's sleep nor the sunrise helped him find the beginning of an answer to that question.

CHAPTER FOUR

The following morning Me'el tried to take a step, but her pain was stronger than her will, and she had to lie down again. She did not want the others to realize it. She needed some time to recover from that blow. She was losing heat minute by minute and she tried to get it back by using her foot. Overcoming fear, she tried to move it, but it was of no use, her foot offered no support. Injuries are like that, they do hurt more the next day. Discouraged, Me'el let herself fall back and stayed there until she got fed up. On top of it all she was wasting time and there was work to be done. Her agitation made her sweat and that only aggravated the pain. Her moaning woke up Anita.

"What is it? Is something wrong?" stirring her rounded body on the straw mat.

"Nothing, child," was the reply. She wanted to say something like, it's just that I am old, but thought better of it and kept quiet. Anita did not dare break the silence. Finally she just had to and asked, "What did you dream about, Me'el?"

"I did not dream. I know nothing about where or how he is, nothing, I did not dream anything."

ᬅᬅᬅᬅᬅᬅᬅᬅᬅᬅᬅᬅᬅᬅᬅᬅᬅᬅᬅᬅᬅᬅᬅᬅᬅᬅᬅᬅᬅᬅᬅᬅᬅᬅᬅᬅ

That wasn't possible. Where could Santiago be? Anita finally realized that Santiago had been away too long. Until then she had not worried about it. Apparently she was in no great hurry to see him and was counting on Me'el being able to find him. An unruly girl like herself could never accomplish that but an older woman like Me'el who knew many people that had passed away only had to ask them and they would tell her. It was her experience that counted, that and the logical order of her reasoning.

Nevertheless, on finding herself disabled, Me'el was crying. For once she thought that her time had come, like fruit past ripe, or the summer ending, with winter on the way. No one could help her. Anita didn't see how she could do anything and was unable to find the right words to console her. But she did attend to her pleas and got up to concoct a pain remedy.

Anita got up without wanting to. She always did everything slowly, particularly in the mornings when she moved around even more slowly. She was used to the grandmother getting up before anyone else to begin the chores. By the time Anita opened her eyes, the tortillas were usually already made. Anita, on the other hand, was never in a hurry. Even today she got up slowly and without any rush at all blew on the fire to prepare the medicine. Since we cannot feel the pain of others there was no reason for her to rush now either.

Me'el let herself down again carefully. She hurt all over. More painful spots kept appearing in parts of her body that she didn't even know existed. Yesterday the pain from her ankle had diverted her attention from other discomforts. A night's rest had only weakened her and revealed to her how serious her condition was. Fully conscious of it now she pleaded with all her heart for the pain to pass.

"Please daughter, pass me the pox."

Anita passed the bottle over to Me'el who straightened herself up for a drink. That was how Anita realized how much Me'el was suffering. Without saying a word, she gave her some tea. Her mother-in-law held on to the little pewter cup. The liquid was sweet. It calmed her down and warmed her blood a bit. She wanted help but had no idea how to ask for it. Never before had she asked for help and now she was even begging for her sins to be forgiven.

She began to confess. Barely whispering, she spoke about her mistakes. She brought back shameful memories and repented with all her soul. The images were getting mixed up and they were being divided. Guided by her conscience and desperate not to lose her soul, she vehemently implored.

"Stay with my body, secret of life. Soul, do not abandon me. Do not leave me alone Holy Mother, Divine Father, flowers, songs, and tears. I cannot beg if there is no forgiveness. I cannot supplicate if there is no mercy. Don't ignore my tears, Holy Mother,

Holy Father. Don't ignore my cries, they are mine, your humble little splinter. Pardon me, for a moment, forgive me, just for a moment," and she closed her eyes, trying not to feel the pain.

Micaela had already gotten up and had begun her chores as she usually did. To her surprise, Anita already had the fire going. She got up close to the water kettle over the fire and Anita told her in a low voice that Me'el was worse off than yesterday. Micaela had had a foreboding and had not slept because of it. This seemed to be a decisive blow.

"Do you feel bad, Me'el?"

"It will go away. It has to." She answered.

Micaela could not stop worrying. She had to seek help, because they were not going to be able to cure her by themselves. They had to call the pulse reader.*

She took down the bar they used every night to close off the doorway and followed the lane to the village center. She was in a hurry and was walking

---

* pulsador; traditional maya therapist that gets most of his information from the characteristics of the pulse.

Chapter IV

fast because she had to do something. She couldn't help but note the dazzling splendor of the sun. Even though the morning light was gleaming in her eyes she could not avoid noticing that a joyous and pretty day had emerged amidst its brilliance and sparkle. The dry cornfield served as a carpet for the sunshine. Admiring the intense green background of the countryside and the dried brown stubble, Micaela kept sinking her bare feet into the mud and with shorter and quicker steps, headed toward the house of don Miguel.

When she got there she didn't dare go in. It was very early and she couldn't see if someone was still sleeping in the room. She waited bashfully outside the door for a moment, but they had noticed her arrival so an invitation to come in sounded immediately.

"Come in, comadre, don't feel bad about finding us still half- asleep."

Dona Chusita was a comadre of Micaela's ever since Manuel's baptism, so they had a good relationship.

"Thank you Comadre. I came to take a little pozol here with you." She took the pozol,without mentioning the reason for her visit, and calmly waited for Chusita to begin the conversation. Chusita had little to talk about, so she brought up the weather. There were still frosts. She heard say that in Chanal the woods were bitten by the frost. It still wasn't clear what the rains would do to the corn this year. That was an anxiety that everybody shared.

षषषषषषषषषषषषषषषषषषषषषषषषषषषषषषषषषषषषषषष

"As to everything else, Comadre, there is nothing new, thank God."

"And my Compadre Miguel, how is he?"

"He is gone. He had to leave five days ago to take a sick person's pulse and it's not clear when he will return. You see, Comadre,* it takes two days to reach the place in the country side where his Uncle Manuel works. It seems that one of his nieces there is the one that isn't well. So he could still be a long way away from where he will undertake the cures. The pulsing** may take some three or four days also, plus another few days for him to return. So when your Compadre may be back is unknown. Do you want something?"

"It's that Me'el is also sick. They already rubbed her and she is not better. She messed up her foot. What a bad time we are going through now, so alone. We would be grateful if my compadre could do us the favor of giving us his opinion."

"I will tell Miguel about it. Do not worry about that. I am keeping your message here, dear Comadre. I myself will make sure that it gets to him. I cannot promise it will be soon, but your message stays safe here with me. And now, Comadre, are you going to tell me that my Compadre Santiago isn't back yet?"

"Well, he is still away."

---

* Comadre or compadre a person who baptizes another persons child assuming responsibility for the child should his parents perish.
** Pulsation diagnosis based on studying the symptoms from the characteristics of the pulse.

"You still have no news from him?"

"No, we don't." She answered slowly and while saying it, she realized that it was not knowing about how he was that bothered her the most. If she knew he was well, she could wait for him all life long.

"Don't worry so much, old friend, what if he is just making out somewhere, you know how it is now that he is carrying money. He will be back, he will return as soon as he gets over the liquor. You know how men are. They leave, but they come back. They always come back, but right now, since he has money he may just have gone on a spree."

She wanted to console Micaela. She tried to tell her that Santiago was well. Instead, she hurt Micaela's feelings very deeply. But it just could not be. Santiago had to come back. He had left everything waiting, her, the children, his responsibilities, and the cornfield unplanted. Everything was unattended to and he knew it. How could he have forgotten his mother that way, their children, herself, even Ana and her little one, and the one she was expecting which he didn't even know about. He had left too many people at home for him not to be missing its warmth, a house made with his own hands, with his fireplace, his roof and his work. He had to be missing his homeland. How could he forget them and stay out so long just for another woman? He would have already brought her home, like Micaela herself, like Anita. It could be that Santiago could still meet another woman, but if a man gets a woman, he takes her, he has to take her, that is what his house is for and Santiago did not abandon his women. Besides, he was a man. He could do whatever he wanted, and after being away from home for so long, men are always looking around, but they come back. They all come back and Santiago had to come back.

Micaela knew she had no right to be checking out her husband so much. Santiago himself would not have allowed it. Too many ideas were beginning to course through her head for her heart to stay in control of them, ideas that were like the mud covering her feet, all mixed up just like her and she couldn't seem to understand herself. She began to put her thoughts in order and saw that she was worrying about uncertainties. She knew that Santiago could not forget about them that easily. Men do leave, but not for long. They always come back, especially when their house is warmed up with the smell of hot beans.

There had to be some other reason behind this. Maybe he was sick or was engaged in some special commitment? Perhaps he was fine, just picking up a few more pennies in order to be with her. But Micaela did not trust her luck. No one before had come back with much money from the finca. Micaela did not lie to herself. Hunger had taught her to get rid of that bad habit since she was a child. She bade farewell to her comadre without the usual formalities and with short steps, trotted back to her own house. She was so eager to arrive that she was tired out from her speedy passage through the village. She was out of breath and sweating when she reached her own oak door.

"You're back already. Any word about Santiago?" Me'el asked at once since she was more concerned about her son than about the pulse taker.

"Nothing," answered Micaela and that explained why she had returned so quickly.

She made no comment about her talk with don Miguel's wife. Micaela had already thought about it and forgotten the possibility that he could just be somewhere drinking. He had been out for too long, he would have already come back in order to recover. Micaela almost preferred that that be the reason why he hadn't come back. She almost wanted him to show up with another woman, just as long as he did show up.

"Did you settle things with don Miguel?"

"I left word. He needs to finish seeing another sick person."

Me'el already knew she had to wait. Even more so if don Miguel was going to take care of her, he had so many people to care for. He was always busy. Sometimes the treatments are simple but even those can take a few days. Then you must always let the pulse expert rest up a little, because he gets tired too.

Me'el took things calmly, as was her nature. She settled herself against the adobe wall, staring at the street. She spent the whole afternoon there sitting on the trunk of a tree, on the threshold and in the shade of the porch. She studied the landscape. It was a squared off map, the outline of a brocade embroidered with the history of her people. She saw Nicolas arrive on the path of the morning sun with his water jars on the back of his burro. She saw doña Antonia arrive with her wood towards the middle of the day and she waited for Maria Rosa to gather in the hens in the shadow of the afternoon.

Meanwhile, the two young girls, sentenced for life to the task of constant house cleaning, resented that Me'el was not able to help with the chores. Anita went along as usual, in her lazy way. That was the way it was with Anita. The more anyone needed her, the more difficult she became. Micaela knew her ways and avoided discussions, but as another day started and knowing that she would not help her, Micaela began to despair.

"Hurry, child it's time to get to work." Anita never hurried. "Look child get going." Anita seemed to not be listening.

"You already could have had the fire started, a little bit of tortilla made. You could have been good for something."

Anita was not very tolerant and let no one offend her.

"Calm down now. No one orders me around."

" Shut up. Get out of here. You're good for nothing."

Chapter IV

Micaela, without thinking twice, hit her. Little Tom ought not to have come over to play with her right then, just when anything would have upset his mother. He wanted to pretend he was a little dog and he hung onto her skirt. But Micaela was not playing. She pushed him away and told him not to bother her.

Tom was too young to know what to do. He had never seen his mother that way, she never shouted. She only punished him when he didn't do what he was supposed to. Otherwise, she never scolded him. Micaela never ran out of patience for her kids.

Tom couldn't even recognize her. When she struck him he even doubted that she had really hurt him. When she recovered, the child had forgotten and accepted her apologies. This had not happened before so he pardoned her immediately. They sat by the doorway and Tom let Micaela hold him for a long time.

She calmed down and went into the house. Anita had been working because the meal was for her also. There always was work to do, the chores were never finished and every drop of water had to be carried in on their heads. Micaela was washing the dishes and Anita was pressing tortillas. Me'el was the only one with nothing to do. She was discouraged and was watching them, as in prison, from an opened door, ironically facing the East.

Me'el watched the landscape that she had seen every day of her life and had never grown tired of it. She knew it by heart but discovered anew the symmetry of the picture in front of her, the play of greens among the dried brown stubble left over in the cornfield from last year that repeated itself, constantly designing a new brocade for her to write with her loom.

She saw the stalks that were standing upright and the ones that were bent over. They were being punished for not having produced corn. Me'el enjoyed the blurred view that her old eyes managed to pick up. The brown rectangles defined the different shades of green, infinitely varied and all of them green. The view from the doorway was always fascinating and was never tiring. She was just watching the scenery until a touch on her shoulder by Domingo interrupted her.

He was so affectionate that Me'el put him on her lap to hold him and check out his hair right away.

"Your ways are nice, dear child! Come over and I will tell you what once happened to a little shepherd just like you. One day, minding his business, just peacefully watching his beloved little lambs graze, he did not notice that he had wandered away from the road leading home. That was how the little boy got lost. Oh, how his parents cried for the little one thinking that he might have fallen into the hands of the evil Owner of the Earth.* That accursed being had passed

---

* *A character similar to the boogey man who rides a deer, uses a snake as a whip and resembles a Spanish conqueror.*

by riding his stag which can only look straight ahead because its eyesight is blocked by two iguanas. That is how the animal is always kept under control. The little boy saw that he was fierce with his whip or better said a viper that he used as a whip and with it snatched the little boy away. Iron fittings were put on his little feet, making him know that until he did not wear them down with hard work he would not know what it is to have bare feet again. This man is evil, pot bellied like all Kaxlán, with a blond beard and great skill in frightening people. When he wants something, he blows gigantic lightning rods from inside the caves where he lives. The lightning shocks you with tremendous thunder."

"So you, Domingo, who can't see well, always take great care not to go the wrong way. How evil the man must be if he can eat the flesh of little lambs, even little sweet ones he has played with and whose wool he has worn. You must take great care of your animals so the man doesn't grab them. It always hurts to lose a little pet that you have loved and worked hard to take care of."

Domingo listened attentively to his grandmother's words. Yes, it was necessary to know how to protect oneself from the Owner of the Earth. That was the reason why he was sitting quietly on Me'el`s lap until the story was over. Actually his grandmother was trying to keep him still so as to be able to go through his hair. She was looking for the lice and nits that nested there. That was a necessary pastime because it was the only way of getting rid of the little creatures that sought out the heat of a body. Domingo's head was the only job that was left for Me'el. She sifted through her grandson's heavy locks, but found nothing. He ought to have been covered with a great swarm of creatures, as he was continually scratching himself and hadn't played in the river for some time. Me'el went through the little black scalp once more and again found not a single nit. Why then did he scratch so much? Tom appeared and made a comment while passing by:

"Domingo sure has a good amount of creatures there."

Finally Me'el knew what was happening. She could not even see the nits and much less a quick moving louse. How could she see anything with weak and tired eyes? She was no longer going to be able to help, not even that job could be entrusted to her, while she spent days sitting on the porch.

Now who was going to help Micaela do all the chores if she was useless? Me'el barely had enough strength to get through the afternoon the way it was. She was not even going to be able to spend her spare time clearing out the heads of the children. How many afternoons had she spent that way, busy sliding off the nits, while they all chatted in the doorway watching the sunset?

Since she couldn't carry water or gather wood, and with such stiff hands now she would not even be able to weave her own cotton shirts or fine brocades. She did try to keep up making tortillas. Micaela had to finish them, but at least Me'el was able to shape them with her hands, without, of course, the speed of former times. Why hurry if all she had to do was to make a few tortillas? She, who used to make them so fast that the children could not keep up with her and even managed to pile them up as they eagerly consumed them, was useless now. Back then she had so much to do. She had to be quick with the tortillas because to begin with there was always a lot of clothing to be washed.

All her troubles seemed to ram into each other suddenly and she began to cry about them. Her first outburst was so violent that Domingo felt embarrassed and took off. Anita saw her through the doorway, but was neither frightened nor worried and she continued braiding her hair.

Micaela put down the kettle of boiling corn that she carried in her hands and went over to see why her mother- in-law was crying that way. She was alarmed. She had to be hurting a lot, because she never complained of pain. She tried to console her, just by being with her at that moment.

Micaela was so worried that she put aside her own problems and gave up trying to be understood also. Almost everything now depended on her strength and she counted on her own integrity. She had always had to give out more than she took in. A routine based on necessity had forced her to it. Ever since Lorenzo was born, she got used to not being able to count on her own time and she forgot about herself. Such neglect speeded up a merciless wear and tear. Now even Me'el required attention.

Every minute there were new problems to deal with. Micaela wanted to guess the future, know what was coming. She wanted to anticipate problems in order to be ahead of them and not have to deal with things one by one, day after day. Overwhelmed by the pressures, she rubbed Me'el's forehead to bring her a little peace. Me'el appreciated it as if it came from one of her own children. It was the first time in her life that she had resigned herself to being an object of compassion.

Anita on the other hand kept walking around and thinking that Me'el deserved what had happened to her. Why did she go away and fall anyway? Now who was going to do her chores? She hoped God wanted her to get better, otherwise how was Me'el going to be able to keep on living this way, like a sack?

Just the fact of hearing her complaining annoyed Anita, who even found the old woman's sobbing repugnant. Why wait for Santiago if she was not even his first woman, because she wasn't his first wife, a real first wife. Why wait without knowing when he might arrive and in the meanwhile do her mother-in-law's chores while watching over so many children of Micaela?

She had to take care of her son and had to rest on account of her condition but why wait around if she now had somewhere to go? Don Antonio had already offered her food and a place to stay. Secretly and silently she began to talk with him.

Ana thought about their last conversation on the bed of dry leaves, there in the woods, away from other people, where she usually met with don Antonio. He said it was becoming difficult for him to live without her. He wanted to be able to begin every morning caressing her. It was hard to have to say goodbye after making love. He needed her in his house so he could eat good tasting food and dress elegantly. Anita was left with the dilemma of having to choose between two lives. She was going to wait for Santiago and decide then. She wanted to remember what Santiago was like. Why continue seeing Antonio under so much stress? It would be so easy to leave with him. Of course, she preferred living with these uncertainties than giving up on seeing him altogether. The feeling that there was something amiss was uncomfortable, because for sure her walks on the mountainside with don Antonio were out of the realm of public approval. As it was, when they saw each other, Ana did not give it much thought. They simply met. When she was in front of don Antonio, Santiago did not exist. Only the feeling of a man's desire for her existed and she could not avoid it. There were no reasons, just odors and sensations since it was what his manliness provoked with brazenness and worldly excitement.

Unable to control the force that drove her to the forest with don Antonio, she went there knowing that she was carrying Santiago's other child. To abandon him while she waited for his second baby was impossible. Don Antonio was in a great hurry to take her away so that Santiago would not snatch her from his side after the infant was born. That way the child would grow up thinking he was his father and not his stepfather. He wanted that woman that much.

CHAPTER FIVE

Micaela brought a plate of beans over to Me'el so she could have a good breakfast. She had a bit of everything, eggs, cheese, beans, in other words, everything. Me'el ate well now that she could since it would be a while before she could eat again because at some time that morning no later than noon, the pulsing had to begin.

As soon as he arrived, don Miguel knew that it was a very serious case since she was an older woman. Consequently, he did not show up alone, but sought help from don Diego, who had more experience and was even older than him.

And the prayers began. They prayed four days before the cross of the house, then just the same way, in front of the crosses on the hills. Me'el fasted from then on. From the moment the sun rose in the morning and all during its daylight splendor, she heard the chorus giving voice to the first prayer. She waited until the first candles burned out and the air became heavy with incense. Me'el kept herself, as always, humble, generous and totally silent.

She wanted her therapists to take notice of it. She offered them a drink for inspiration, for better communication with her and with the Saints. Only that way could the truth be known and an accurate diagnosis made. Me'el called upon St. Thomas and the rest of the Saints in heaven. She wanted to be cured.

Finishing his first drink, don Miguel took up Me'el's fist and concentrated on feeling the rhythm of her pulse. He took a long time. He paid attention to her eyes, the tone of her skin, and he felt her agitated pulse, it was steady, beating rapidly and was warm. It proved life was in her. After hearing her heart and feeling her soul, don Miguel was truly alarmed. He found her spirit firmly rooted in the past and felt the pulse of her nomad walk into the future. He pressed her wrinkled skin, felt it, and there was no longer any doubt. Pieces of her soul were missing. This was much more ominous than a fall.

Don Miguel stepped back from her side without saying a word. He did not want to prejudice don Diego who was coming over to form his own opinion. He proceeded calmly. He looked her over carefully. He took her arm and then seized her wrist. Her blood was rushing too fast. Hers really was a serious case. At that point he asked that a third pulse expert be brought in. They were going to need more help.

The children took off to see if they could locate don Pedro. Everyone else stayed quietly there with Me'el, keeping her company, as well as each other because not only do the sick and the dead need sympathy, but the living that surround them, the ones who stay behind, depend on it too.

All the participants made themselves comfortable on the porch under the roof with the broad shingles to talk things over calmly. The bottle passed from hand to hand while Micaela told them all the details of Me'el's fall.

"Thank you," she said, taking the liquor, "Thank you too for being with us. Santiago will be grateful to you. I can still remember looking at Me'el's face, full of fear, as she lay there on the ground. Her face was covered with fear. I saw it myself. I saw the fear she bore.

Don Diego and don Miguel gave their opinions and they agreed.

"If it were just the injury, your mother-in- law would already have been well. Our concern is that fear's frightened part of her soul away that's why the injury to her foot does not go away. Otherwise her foot would have gotten better by now.

"Everything is worse now because she's scared and since she is afraid she can't get better. She has to be in peace, forget her fears, calling her soul to return from the earth and then quickly look for her lost nahual. You should hurry and look for it soon, because many days have gone by after her fall. It is far a way for sure by now so it's going to be hard to find it. Of course whether or not it is lost depends upon luck, since she is old so it may well be lost. It could easily have gone far away and be lost."

"But look, Micaela, when a nahual is used to being with us, it is difficult for him to take off. It knows where it belongs, after so many years of being in just one heart. There are cases in which the little lost creature does get lost, but later returns."

It was better to suppose that that was the case. They hoped that Me'el's good luck was intact and her nahuales had not yet departed from her well-built corral. It is hard for a creature to jump over a well -made fence. However, in a situation as complicated as this one, it was better to rely upon one more opinion. The children who went to look for don Pedro came back right away. He would be there soon and his support would be very useful.

They had already made up their minds by the time he arrived. Don Pedro readied himself to listen to the earlier stories. An excess of pox was interfering with the orderly flow of scientific information. Don Pedro took in the liquor, along with a diagnosis that was already determined. By the time he pulsed Me'el the criteria had been dictated. He warmed up with a little more drink and went over to feel her blood flow.

As he got close he smelled the flowers that were used in tidying up her bed. He took her hand and felt her pulse. It ran so fast that he had no doubt that her temperature was elevated. He checked its flow and, having managed to acquire as much data from her blood as possible, he moved over to one side to offer an opinion.

"The blow was quite hard, that is clear, and, with her fright, there is little improvement. I do not believe that it was the fright that sent her soul away, but that she fell because it was already lost. If someone wanted her to fall, then she had to fall. It would be good to find out who might have wanted this misfortune to take place. As to her foot, all she needs is to leave it alone and keep it still by attaching some boards or branches to it, fixed just right so it can't move, at least until the pain is gone. Right now, what we need to take care of more urgently is that heat in the blood stream, so it doesn't cause her to lose her mind."

Don Miguel spoke. "What I disagree on is that I believe that it was the fall alone that took away her spirit."

Don Diego was the only one who had not offered an opinion. He was in agreement to some extent with the other two, mediating between their two views. He couldn't determine the exact origin of the misfortune but did know that her soul was in danger. Something had to be done soon but where to begin? No one knew anyone who could have wanted to hurt her. They did have to get to the bottom of this, but in the meantime there was something much more urgent to attend, the fall itself.

As they never came to a single view, they went on to take her pulse again. They only managed to lose time, as their opinions did not change and the diagnostic process was not moving ahead. The doctors took some corn and they spoke to the dry kernels one by one. They asked where they could find the old woman's soul, where even just a little piece of it might be.

Don Diego dropped some kernels into the salted water. They carefully blew on the corn a little, holding it firmly with their hands stretched out. A white kernel fell, then a red one and then a black one. Yet not one yellow kernel sank to the bottom of the gourd. Three kernels did sink and three shamans saw how the kernels took their places, thereby giving honor to the Holy Trinity and sending hope from the corn. Sinking, because of their weight and soaking up the salted water, the chosen grains that were illuminated by burning torches represented those parts of her soul that were still with her, the ones that were not missing. There were several. There was only a small piece wandering lost among the unknown.

It might have been the dim light, or perhaps the excess of alcohol, that enabled them to settle so much in favor of her recovery. In fact, there was little that was precise about the arrangement of the kernels and they were relying too much on their hopes. The ambiguities offered consolation, less than half of her spirit appeared to be lost. Only fragments had gone off. Therefore, they now went on to begin the real cure, the call to what had been lost.

The corn kernels fell into the next jar and were presented before the cross in the patio that protected the house. And the prayers followed. All together so they could be stronger and louder. They solemnly asked for the liberation of her soul that was being held fast and manipulated by that grimly Owner of the Earth.

Me'el's spirit was strengthened because she knew that she had never done harm to anyone. She had never even wished evil upon anyone. Of course, she had never touched anything that belonged to the Owner of Everything, that vile denizen of the caves.

"Come on out now," cried the chorus, "Come now from wherever you have been in the earth, from wherever you were, all alone bundled up. Come out from wherever you were frightened, from where you got anxious, even your feet got scared and your hands got scared also. Close to you, right before you The Divine Mother and the Holy Father are with you. They are all with you, your sacred ancestors and their minions. With their feet and their divine hands too, they are beside you. Now come, come to Me'el. You cannot stay there stretched out, face down just because you left that way, you ran away frightened from that place, as though you were distressed in such a place. Wherever you are, wherever you go, be it up or down, remember your home. Now come, come to Me'el."

One puff over the kernels showed the direction that her soul was taking. The corn went around in a complete circle and don Miguel turned in every direction to find it. He stamped the ground and demanded an answer. He blew in the gourd that sounded like a whistle. The piercing noise called out to what was lost so it could follow the call and might find its way home to the pen. Me'el had prepared the corral by decorating it with flowers. Flowers were strewn around her bed and throughout the house so that the lost soul might want to come back to where it was loved so much, back by Me'el's side.

Don Miguel took the old woman's arm, breathing over the locations where the pulse is felt most distinctly, and called out to the blood. He called again for the blood to run and carry her soul along with it, so as to nourish her body. They used the sign of the holy cross to seal off the most vulnerable parts of her skin. Four crosses, sketched out with the blood of a chicken they were going to cook for her, covered her wrists and her upper forearms. All the exits were sealed. Her soul would not escape again. Now protected by the Holy Cross, painted with a red geranium used as a brush, they fortified the four cardinal points where the beat of life can be felt.

The four extremities of the cross were there, represented by the four colors of corn, leaving only one point vulnerable and unprotected, the one that should have been protected by the yellow kernels.

Again they bathed her wrist and again the middle part of her arms, with the secret of life, blood, the blood that once had flown freely in accord and harmony with the rhythm of time, under the black feathers nourishing in all the hidden corners of the body with powerful magic, now turned into meat. From body to mind, from habit to reasoning, the sacred liquid marked the difference between life and death.

Me'el bathed her feet with flowers drenched in water. She drank the blood from the chicken and gave away the flesh, now bereft of its black plumage. The flesh was so thin it was worthy of being served at the altar as an offering. This was how they tricked the Owner of the Earth, who was distracted by devouring a good meal, and so became prone to give up whatever he had in his hands. Me'el's nahuals could then escape and return to the protection of her body. Once the nahuals manage to break free, their home attracts them and they return. Me'el patiently waited for their return, there under the blankets washed with waters of white lilies and orchids. Used to waiting, since she had never been in a hurry, Me'el waited for them to come back.

They might move about if they are lost, but with God's help, the little creatures have to come back. Lost that way on the mountain, they have to feel hunger and that makes them come home, it makes us all come back. With great assurance, Me'el prepared her bed for them and surrounded it with flowers.

It was an inviting nest. If she called out from there to the nahuales or her relatives just like her on the mountain, they would have to return. Patiently she waited to be cured. She was confident that someday her pain would go away. Her heart prayed in the Holy name of Mary and in the name of the Lord who is omniscient and sets all measure. She pleaded for Their peace first, that They be well, that They be in a state of Sanctity, that They find Themselves in a state of Holiness, if that were possible, of course, and so gain relief from suffering and above all, be dispensed from death.

"Look how I suffer, how weak I am. My humble back lacks protection. My humble side is just the same way without protection. One afternoon, one morning, I was without protection, your protection. Holy Mother, Divine Father, if you can, if I deserve it, give me your protection back."

Me'el saw Micaela busy getting food ready for the healers, and she was distressed not being able to help her. Now there was even more work and it was her fault. Micaela kept the house in order now that Me'el was sick. There was more work than just the daily sweeping, because anything done for Me'el required special preparations. She needed the purest water, from its source in the high mountain. Micaela soaked white lilies in that water to finish purifying it. The corral where Me'el waited for her spiritual companions to return could only be sterilized with flowers that grow among the trees on the sacred mountains, magnificent gardens of all that is divine.

Micaela had prepared everything for the ceremony. She had swept the road to make way for the sun and the pulse takers. She had fulfilled all the requirements for purification and asepsis. She bathed Me'el with the water of drenched mountain flowers. As a good patient, disabled by her bad luck, she accepted the relaxing bath with gratitude.

Me'el had no need to ask what would happen next. She knew how sick people were cured and knew that the doctors continued drinking and eating to be able to keep on with the cure for several days. Everything depended on the divinity because chance disposes of life according to whim, but the divine imposes order. When two worlds are believed to exist, the living and the dead, they are confused and they are often found in the same place at the same instant. Therefore, one has to drink in order to be able to feel, since man is not all thought. He is both reason and heart. Rapture from inebriation adds feeling to reason. It brings out the truth and compelled the pulse experts to engage Me'el's pain.

Before leaving for the crosses in the hills, don Miguel left the liquor at the head of Me'el's corral to make sure that the ones who stayed behind to watch over the house did not fall asleep. The children took care of it. They gave the house another sweeping. It was an intense moment, and that was the only thing they could do for Me'el. Vulnerable as she was, they wanted to help her, and so they looked after their house in order that no misfortunes would visit her cradle. Others, helping Me'el, went off together to the crosses, to the highest temples or, as it were, to the most lofty summits where they had to keep on praying. The pilgrims left from the house trying to beat the sun before it ended its journey. They took a way that lead them in the direction contrary to the path of the sun, as if trying to overtake time, and then hold it suspended, stretching the hour, until the old woman could leave her pain in the past.

They placed the curtain of candles in front of the first cross. The little lights were flickering, casting confusion over the offering and hiding it from the view of witches, preventing them thereby from taking advantage of their weakness by stealing the humble offering. The guardian candles burned, the gods were consuming them until they were spread over the ground like offerings of tortillas. Everybody prayed in the sanctuary, there on the summit in the divine name of Jesus Christ, the Lord.

"Take this then, My Lady and Divine Father that both of you are. I have come on my knees I have come humbly to your lordly side. Receive this and let me step and walk at your feet, below your hands, in other words here in the sanctuaries of your mountains. If you accept this in grace, if you think well of me, this vile little thing, your humble splinter,

🔲🔲🔲🔲🔲🔲🔲🔲🔲🔲🔲🔲🔲🔲🔲🔲🔲🔲🔲🔲🔲🔲🔲🔲🔲🔲

then accept these four meager pine branches, these few candles from me, your daughter and nursling. Take this humble incense, this humble bit of smoke from me, your daughter, your own child. I implore your divine pity and ask for your divine forgiveness."

The bottle of liquor passed from hand to hand. They worshiped the crosses the same way each blade of new corn is venerated. They left there an offering of chicken facing the East. With its head toward the sun, and with a carpet of pine needles separating heaven from earth, they marked the four cardinal points, the four corners of the cosmos, and then they returned to the house for supper. They paused for a last time as they passed by the cross that blessed the door way. They offered some candles and honest words so they could eat in peace.

Not surprisingly, the mealtime conversation would turn into a prolonged after dinner event. Micaela offered them what she had to eat. It was no banquet, but her tortillas, egg, and beans, seasoned with smoke of the wood, were tasty. They ate no chicken so that some would be left for Me'el for the sake of her recovery. One had already been consumed that morning and the other was sacrificed for her lunch, leaving one chicken for the Owner of the Earth. Fortunately, they still had corn and beans from the sale of the little pig.

Don Miguel personally undertook the sacrifice of the chicken to evaluate the results of the treatment.

He was disappointed, the creature twisted around to the West till it died. Aware of the bad omen that it was, don Diego sadly took up the chicken and straightened it out toward the East without telling Me'el anything about this. Micaela served the blood to Me'el, who took and drank the broth along with the thankful feeling of relief that nursing brings. Grandma wasn't lonely, since no one left that night. But the shamans were uneasy because they were committed to assuring her recovery. They would never just leave her in the hands of fate.

CHAPTER SIX

Things went back to normal. The healers had left, and chores were still there, as they always were. The only thing that had not gotten back to normal was Me'el's foot. The process of curing had been peaceful and had taken place in an orderly, patient fashion, but even so, it had not worked. Her foot was so inflamed it was still deformed.

Me'el did not complain. She said very little, measuring her words more than ever, especially her complaints. This sore was not going away. It seemed like it wanted to stay with her until she died. From now on whatever she had to do, whatever she had to struggle for, she would have to go through lame as she was. She had no other choice, other than to keep on living and hope that time might clear up her situation. Meanwhile, she filled every afternoon with patience and felt the pleasure of watching the little ones. That's how she cheered up the sunsets, in spite of her inevitable anxiety about Santiago.

Micaela concentrated on her housework. Why go around with a wandering mind, when it is better to focus on the tasks at hand? She had to take care of the washing. She gathered up the dirty clothes and all her little ones. Each one carried something, Tom grabbed the soap, because it weighed less, Domingo took his dirty pants, and the girls mounted two wooden tubs of clothes on their heads as they went off to the river to help out with the wash.

Micaela put her hand in the water and took out another garment. It was the blouse she used every day, the one with broad, white lace and a low neck with many stags embroidered by her own hands with the cross stitch. Her oval neckline, falling loose on her shoulders, was different from that of the other women of Cuxulja, because almost all of them had come with their families from Oxchuc looking for land to settle down on, but she was born near Ocosingo and had come to Cuxulja through marriage so wore a Tzeltal outfit from a warmer land.

She rubbed homemade soap into it, like the soap she made as a child from a firm household, a family similar to the one she cared for now, large, all raised in a house like her own, with a fire place to cook on in the middle. She placed the shirt on a rock in the river that was smooth from years of use and she applied more soap. She scrubbed, rinsed and wrung it out, dipping it in the clear water that ran by. Micaela saw the white foam go off with the current, until there were no more white particles given off by the linen making the clear water hazy. She kept the blouse in the river so the current would do some of the work. Looking up, she enjoyed the landscape. She watched the deep narrow river slicing through the underbrush, invaded now by a bevy of children bathing themselves in the sun's heat.

It was not difficult to wash on a day like this, with the sun bright and the water warm. On the other hand, when the water is cold, you're hands feel like they are full of splinters. But now Micaela was enjoying her task. It was all she asked for, to be able to tan her skin while watching the little ones play, doing what she had to do employing and enjoying the vigor of her youth.

She was doing two jobs at once, making sure the children were safe and also getting the wash done. She wanted to get some soap on the kids, but knew they would resist. She hoped that the heat might tempt them to soak themselves close to her. Micaela took advantage of every opportunity she had to wash their faces when they came near. With games and tricks, she even ended up washing their hair.

But little Tom was too busy. He was losing the bicycle tire he was running next to, pushing it with a stick, up and down over the uneven ground. The tire rolled along in front of him and he shouted as he ran, putting it back up again and guiding it between rocks and shrubs, according to his whim. He moved quite gracefully for a boy only four years old. Dark skinned and practically blond from playing so much in the sun, he made continual noises as he tried to keep his tire upright.

"Ba ba, sum, sum, sum, kuu, naa, kuu." It was a steep hill.

Domingo came out of the thicket and ran over to Tom with a husk in his hand. It was his weapon, a machete and it was an ambush against Tom. With a surprise attack he took the tire away. All at once, Tom saw his tire going off under Domingo's control who shouted;

"Come on! You little jerk! Take it away from me, if you can!"

Tom realized it was a trick. He ran after his tire to get it back. But Domingo was ahead of him by a rather large advantage by about four steps in meters and four years of age, so Tom's efforts were useless. He crumpled clumsily onto the ground and buried his face. Dirty and angry, he complained to his mother.

"He knocked me down." Tom told her. "Domingo knocked me down."

Micaela dropped her work as soon as she saw his face covered with dirt. She looked for a hidden injury but didn't find any so she then hugged the boy calmly.

"Who do you say pushed you?"

꙳꙳꙳꙳꙳꙳꙳꙳꙳꙳꙳꙳꙳꙳꙳꙳꙳꙳꙳꙳꙳꙳꙳꙳꙳꙳꙳꙳꙳꙳꙳꙳꙳꙳

"Domingo. Domingo knocked me down."

"That's a lie," chorused Domingo in his own defense, and Mariana who had seen it all.

"He didn't even touch him." She said calmly. They were fighting over the tire." Micaela understood, they had to straighten it out themselves.

Mariana knew what she was talking about. She did not have to pretend to be a mother. She already acted like one. She was almost 12 years old and already marked by the signs of maturity that maternal care gives. For almost six years she had been looking after the smaller ones to keep them from hurting themselves. After all she had lived with a little one wrapped in her rebozo since she was five.

"That screwball fell down on his own," said Domingo.

"Yes, he was running along, and he stumbled."

"How did you fall?" asked Micaela, inspecting Tom's face.

"He knocked me down. He took away my tire and threw me down."

"Did he push you? What happened?"

"He made me run after him until I fell."

"Clean your face and do your work. This all happened because you weren't minding your own business. You know that when you aren't paying attention something is bound to happen. Get some wood. There's not enough left for even half a morning. Domingo, leave your little brother alone and go back to your duties. Mariana, help me drain the clothes. Maria Rosa, you too, stop playing and do what you should be doing, like what you are, two grown up girls."

Micaela took the child carefully by the shoulders and headed him to the water. Tom exaggerated and resisted the wash. Micaela won the battle, by neither spanking him, nor letting him go free. She was successful in running clean water over his face. Then with a slight tap on the shoulder she took him carefully to face what had threatened him, the earth. She started out by scolding him saying;

"Can't you see where you put your feet? Do you think that it is right for you to fall on the ground," then she begged the Saint Earth that it not keep the soul of her son and cutting three branches from the closest bush she passed them over him beginning with his right hand, going up his arm, crossing over his body and going down his left leg. She just as carefully repeated the same process starting on his left hand and finishing on his right leg and then tied the three little branches to his back so he could go now, safely on his way.

The girls let go of the flowers they had gathered. Mariana had some for the arrangement of the altar and Maria Rosa, some for her playhouse. The three of them finished up the washing quickly and arranged the wet clothes in the tubs.

With the work done, Micaela, who felt a little warm, got into the water. She slid down the bank near a deep side surrounded by rocks that made little waterfalls and formed a safe pool for her to swim in. Soon she was surrounded by all of her children, at least by the ones who were with her now. The older ones were missing, because they were working in the cornfield and no longer went with her to the river ever since they had become true farmers. Manuel was missing also because he was far away at the boarding school.

Micaela saw them and recalling her own life she could not believe how big they had grown. What would become of them when they were older? She tried to imagine them as adults. The girls would have no problems. They would get married, and until then, they had a home. Domingo was the only one who didn't know where to turn to. He was still there by her side because of pure bad luck. He simply had not been able to pass the entrance exam for the boarding school because of his bad eye sight. They said they had to give the chance to students with better possibilities.

No one knew why the disease had been so cruel with Domingo. His brothers had recovered quickly, but Domingo instead of improving, was getting worse every day. This really hurt Micaela, because she knew how much he would suffer, especially being a boy. Nevertheless, she was grateful for having seven children and that they all were alive. In spite of Domingo's trachoma she thanked God that she was able to see her seven children as often as she did. She was satisfied to see the elder ones two or three times every week, especially now that they had turned out so handsome and tall. The bond between Sebastian and Lorenzo, who were always together, could not have been stronger. They were healthy in body and soul and had everything their way, because they were the ones who would take over Santiago's land. It was not much, but was something and it was land, and with that, their future was assured. Santiago had gone against all tradition and had decided to leave the land to the elder ones because of Domingo. He expected them to take care of him. That is why he did not leave his land to Tom, the youngest, as was usual because he truly believed in his boys. After all they were farmers already.

Domingo, on the other hand, was at the mercy of misery itself. With all hope based on his brothers' future, a void opened up in his own. He depended on the inheritance of his older brothers and on how much Spanish Manuel would learn at his school. Now he was playing excitedly with little Tom, who was everybody's favorite toy.

It was Micaela who insisted that Manuel go to the boarding school so that he would come back reading and able to take care of Domingo. He was the chosen one to go. The elder ones had to help their father. Manuel could go, because he was not going to get any land. They had little enough for Lorenzo and Sebastian. Micaela laid all her trust on him and asked God that he not abandon his brother when Domingo went blind.

On the other hand, Santiago had a deep distrust of all that business. He saw Manuel going away a lot and coming back with new ways. He would have preferred that he stay to work in the cornfield, like the others. But his doubts did not change Manuel's course at all. He did leave for the boarding school anyway and with time, Santiago's suspicions about the boarding school only grew, in the same manner as Manuel began to mistrust his father's words.

Micaela had left the tubs with the clothes slightly tipped to drain in the pasture. With her breasts bronzed by the sun's rays and her skirt tucked up under her sash, she slipped along the riverbank clinging to the underbrush. Intensified by the light, her body tones were accentuated. Her brown complexion stood out in spite of the dark blue skirt that went around her body. The tightly wrapped skirt displayed her narrow waist and formed a single fold in front, tied by a broad, red and joyful sash.

The girls imitated her, and knowing the rules of discretion, they undressed only to the waist, keeping their skirts on with identical sashes and similar folds doubled over their bellies. Later on, they would learn how to adjust it according to the changes of their bodies, because in fact it was an exclusive design for maternity, which for now was just a question of style and was quite feminine.

Micaela came out of the water with her chest pulled in from the cold. The sun's light upon her mature breasts gave an amber-like hue to her nipples, with a slightly reddish tint, like the coloring of the amber of the rarest kind brought back by the men when they returned from the plantations of Simojovel. Her well turned legs, built up from walking so much in the mountains, filled out her narrow skirt that was now wet. She set her feet firmly on the ground to begin smoothing out her shiny black hair, for who knows how many suns Micaela had counted but anyway you counted them, she wasn't a day over 30 years old.

The two girls left the water after she did. Their smooth hairless bodies would always remain so in the future, even the most intimate parts, when the soft hands of a man would caress them. Still girls, they responded like women to the work that had to be done. They gathered the clothes together in the tubs and put them up on their heads. Micaela took up the heaviest and hurried, because she knew that the grandmother was waiting.

Domingo collected his marbles, all "chinese ladies." He had left the kings and the "halfsies" at home and had brought only his less important marbles. But Tom did not want to leave. He wanted to keep on playing in the river. He did another somersault and shouted deliriously with his feet in the air. He kept on turning over again and again, tirelessly. Domingo relished watching him doing turns through the pasture and he did a somersault himself. Micaela ignored them, quite aware that they knew the road home better than she did. She went on ahead with the two young women, carrying the wet clothes on their heads.

Domingo and Tom kept on playing with the tire. It looked like bullfighting, because Tom was charging against him and Domingo made fun of him every time he made a pass. From afar, Micaela saw from Tom's expression that a disturbance was brewing. She realized that a fight was about to begin and just at the moment Tom threw himself on the ground and shouted out the most offensive thing he could say.

"Damn you." he cried out and Micaela, annoyed, went back for them.

She usually did not meddle in their fights, but when they insulted each other so strenuously, she could no longer stay on the sidelines. Her tolerance was at an end. She put down the tub from her head in order to have her two hands free so she could catch them and put them to carrying wood. Unconcerned about who was pinched, Micaela required obedience. She punished both boys and sent them straight on down the road. They quickly tied their harness on around their heads and easily mounted loads of wood on their backs. That was a job they were quite used to.

Micaela proceeded along the path with her little ones in single file behind her. She arrived at the edge of the village and began to go up the hill that took her to the house that Santiago had put up for her. The clothes upon her head were beginning to be very uncomfortable because she knew she had only a few more steps to go. It was not until she put the tub down and felt so relieved from doing it that she realized how heavy it was. When she went in, she found Me'el making tortillas and noted there was that not much dough left. She turned around and saw the pile of tortillas and knew that Me'el, on her own, without mentioning it to anyone was now rationing out the nixtamal.* Her mother- in- law offered her a tortilla as soon as she arrived.

"I'm not hungry, mother, you eat."

"Washing makes you hungry. Take your tortilla, child."

"You eat. Truly, I am not hungry. You and the children eat first."

The children did not think twice about it. When they came in, they went over to the fireplace, which smelled like tortillas. They shared the tortillas and each one of them added salt and chile on theirs.

"Are there any beans?" asked Tom, knowing that they had not had any yesterday so there had to be some today.

---

* cornmeal

"There is cabbage, there is chayote* and there must be some squash out in the vegetable garden." Micaela replied. "There is still enough to eat."

Micaela remembered when she was a child. No one talked about a bad harvest. There were bad seasons, some with less corn than others, but there was always enough corn to be sold. This year, not even Santiago's land, in the East under the early sun, not even the richest lands that faced the sunrise were going to produce much corn.

The elders had clearly predicted that if nobody organized a fiesta for Saint Thomas it was going to be a bad year. The Saint was ofended, but no one could take charge because no one had enough money to offer the kind of party that Saint Thomas deserved. No one could meet the expectations of the people, no celebration could be good enough, without a fiesta for the Saint, this was going to be a bad year for sure. Afterwards, if there is bad weather, the griping begins, and whoever made the party turns out to be guilty because he made such a paltry fiesta for the Saint. Clearly, with everything so expensive, a big festival was impossible since the candles were so expensive, the fireworks even more so and the tortillas so scarce. That was why this year even the few old musicians that remained went off to the fincas, because any fiesta for the Saint would not be good enough.

---

* pear squash, vegetable pear

Only the head men stayed. They kept their word and kept things going because although there would be no first councilman that year, they were all committed to the council. There was an official president who spoke with the authorities. Even though, the rest of them maintained their positions. Santiago did not want to abandon the council, especially now that he was a fourth councilman. He had become accustomed to talking with the headmen and he too was committed to the council. Now a deputy since he had served four times as trustee, after a long term earlier as a mayordomo, when he was young but married already and until then had become a municipal official and was initiated into the affairs of public order.

Not everyone could carry the weight of responsibilities and serve as councilman. Some refused, you have to earn people's confidence. The most worthy of them took on the year as a challenge and kept up with their duties, in spite of the hard times in Oxchuc as had been foreseen by the elders.

Anita came into the house carrying water for her bath. She carried her child, now quite big, in her shawl and her belly had grown also. Soon it would be necessary to attend another birth in the house. Micaela would bring in the water. Me'el, in charge, would assist by urging Anita to be patient, and they would light up the fire to warm up the house. Anita would soon be bringing a second little one into the world in that room and with God's will, it would also be a boy. How wonderful that would be for Anita because boys are always closer to a mother. Micaela, on the other hand, would not be having a child this year. If only Santiago had left her expecting a baby, it would have been easier to wait for him. In any case she had given Santiago two girls that would take care of him in his old age and all the loving he might have wanted from her.

Micaela got splashed from the water thrown on the hot rocks heating on the fire for the steam bath. She saw the mountain of reddened rocks that soon would be covered with water. Then steam warmed up the room covering their bodies and bathing them with their own sweat. Micaela remembered the last time that they fired up a steam bath together, she, Santiago, Me'el, and Anita. The children always came in afterwards because they would wait for the room to cool down a little before coming in. Micaela rested her head on the wall, the steam was relaxing, and with her straight hair loose, her imagination also flew back to the prettiest memory of all, the first time Santiago set up the steam bath for her.

After keeping his promise to put up a house for her, and all the promises he had to make about catering his father-in-law, he returned humbly to her parents every time they asked him to. Inspite of the punishments and scoldings, he was happy. So, after bowing to their wishes every day for a week and promising to bring in the wood for a whole year, did his father-in-law accept the bottles he was giving him. Her parents made him know that if she was not happy with him, she always had a home to come back to. Not until then did they let them get married, and they did, after the gifts for her and her father, and the party and the fireworks.

Micaela laughed nervously when she went into a house alone with a man for the first time. Santiago sensed it and to ease her anxiety, and his, he set up the steam bath, with the idea that being partially undressed as she was used to, things would be easier for her, at least more familiar, because she did know about that kind of nudity, but only that kind of nudity, because not even during the few times they had met among the leaves of the cornfield, was the sash that held her skirt around her waist untied from it. Dressed as she was to wash in the river or to take a steam bath her outfit never changed, it was always the same, with her skirt always tied to her waist, always covered and her breast always exposed, just as her face was. She remembered her skin being caressed and the seemingly accidental close contact that sent pleasure through every part of her body. That afternoon, when she was 15 years old, with no vices in her heart or bad thoughts in her mind, she allowed her body to freely feel pleasure, while Santiago, with so much gentleness, enjoyed his first woman.

With renewed freshness, Micaela remembered the peace and calm that followed that afternoon of love.

She recalled her own words when she told Santiago that she did not want to be in any other place.

"Right here, where I am now, is where I have been most happy. This is my place. Holding you, I am where I should be."

They talked for many hours, gazing at one another and at the fire, the same fire that she was looking at now, in the same room she shared with her seven children. They were all born there, in front of the cooking fire that would be burning for Anita's baby, who would soon be born. The stones would be brazing for the birth of a another little one, and hot steam would be flowing over their skin so they could welcome another son of Santiago.

CHAPTER SEVEN

Anita could not think of anything else. Her belly got bigger and Santiago did not return. She was alarmed now to discover that she didn't miss him. She wanted to go off with don Antonio. They could run away together, to another village. He had offered her bed and breakfast and a place to get away from the gossip. What made things worse was waiting for a child and husband at the same time. She knew that now they needed her more than ever in the house, but she only wanted to have the baby and leave. After all, she could leave as long as she left Santiago's child behind her.

It was surely necessary to leave because everyone would soon be aware of her longings for don Antonio. Anita was afraid of the blows that would certainly sting. Once the scandal surfaced, they would be talking about her. As she walked through the plaza, through the market, everywhere, they would be saying things about her.

Now she had to go fetch the wood. Anita was getting ready to go to gather some up when Micaela offered to go with her. She wanted to walk through the woods. Anita shrugged her shoulders.

"If you want to go, then go. I'll stay here."

"Let's go together. I can't handle all the wood I need by myself," replied Micaela. Anita just turned over and lay on the mat.

"Why do you have such bad manners?" Micaela went on saying, "Do you think that I have to help you with your work? Go and do your chores. I am going with you, in order to help you, not to do your work."

Anita could no longer refuse and she got up. If she insisted too much on staying, Micaela would ask too many questions and it bothered Anita to give out any explanations whatsoever. She got up from the ground and grabbed her pack harness just to keep Micaela quiet.

"Yesterday I found a large pile of sticks over there in the morning shade," she said, trying to keep Micaela on the usual path.

Micaela was used to changing routes and went straight over to the bed of leaves where Ana dallied on a daily basis. Anyone could notice how nervous Anita was, walking along so as not to run into don Antonio, who, like a curse upon her, came out from among the trees without seeing Micaela.

"Why are you so late? I am lucky to find you. I was just about to leave," and without wasting any time began to caress her. He took his liberties, because over the course of a month he had become familiar with every part of her body.

"Get out of here!" Anita shouted at him. "What do you want with me?"

"What's this? Do you feel all right? Don't you love me anymore?"

Anita gave him a burning look. Antonio didn't understand, but Micaela made everything clear by striking him on the head and began pulling furiously at his black hair. Then Micaela scratched him with fury and, without knowing quite how, ended up hitting poor Anita in the face. Frightened, Anita could only cry and let the beating go on. Antonio held Micaela's hands, knowing he shouldn't interfere. He knew she had the right to beat her but he tried to defend her.

"Calm down," he shouted several times until Micaela managed to contain her anger and began to talk about Santiago's honor. Micaela insulted them as much as she could. She shouted at them, and Anita just cried. She had no right to defend herself.

Antonio took advantage of the pause to try to speak calmly, to make her understand many things, but it was impossible. Micaela had never felt the reasons they had for seeing one another.

"Look, Micaela. I'll go if you want, but leave Anita alone. I'll go away, as long as you don't spread this around."

Antonio could imagine the life that awaited Anita. He knew how slanderous people are. Some are thoughtful and comprehensive. They don't interfere with anyone else but there are those who enjoy hurting others. Micaela immediately threatened to tell everybody.

"Let her suffer her punishment. Let her pay for her sin. Let everyone know!"

Micaela could not imagine how much she would have to share Anita's sin and that is why she wanted to hurt Anita as much as possible. And now that Santiago had such a high position, how many people would take advantage of his shame? Once offended, Santiago was going to take revenge on both of them. The children would pay the highest price, one they did not owe. That was the reason Antonio insisted and begged Micaela not to say anything to Santiago. But his plea made Micaela fly into even more of a rage.

"It must be known, or this evil will never go away. The truth must always be seen, because when shame so big is locked up in the heart like this, it gets rotten. The sin rots it. So Santiago has to know."

She forgot the wood she needed so badly and took Anita back home crying. Anita walked along without trying to run away, morally compelled by the torture of her shame.

Me'el remained quiet when the two daughters-in-law came in. She saw Anita be beaten again and had an idea of what it was about. Her old eyes had seen lazy Anita too happy when she went off for the wood. She had always kept quiet about it, leaving it up to Santiago to decide what to do. Me'el could even pretend to be blind if that was called for, or to be deaf if there was something that she was not supposed to hear. It was a dementia acquired at a painful price.

Poor Anita did deserve the cruel treatment. It would have been useless to hold Micaela's hands back anyway. It was better for Micaela to vent her anger once and for all. Me'el knew that Anita would not die from the blows, instead it would ease her conscience a little by taking away some of the remorse. The sense of injustice takes the shame away by balancing both till they level out so the sense of injustice erases the shame and the conscience feels free to forget its sin. She needed that confession. Me'el was afraid that Micaela would be sorry about having been so hard on her, besides, who could know what Anita's revenge would be like. It would be even worse because she knew Anita wouldn't stop, revenge encouraged by spite only reinforces it. Me'el preferred to stay out of this one. She knew that it was Santiago's business and if she got involved, she could have problems with him, especially with Anita being such a liar. She was capable of turning him against them and as a mother there would be nothing she could do. No judge is crueler than a son, no scorn greater than being forgotten by him and no pain can be worse than that. With so much to lose, Me'el could not take the risk. She kept quiet, an easy thing for her to do up till then and she preferred it that way since she couldn't do anything anyway not even stand up for her son's honor. Santiago could move away and then she would only see him when he visited her. It was not worth risking more grief and pain just because of Anita, especially with her life slipping away since heat kept escaping because of the injury of her foot.

She tried to understand Anita even though she did not like her, because after so many years without a husband, she could not get used to it either. She missed her man each morning, every afternoon. She did not judge anybody nor did she feel she had the right to. She wasn't a 'judging' person and she knew what it was to be a young woman. She felt sorry for Anita, but Santiago's honor was first.

"People are going to know about this," warned Micaela. Knowing the punishment she was imposing, she stopped hitting Anita. Her arm hurt her from beating her so much. Me'el decided to interfere.

"What the people who live in this house do, is only the business of those who live in this house. What people who share the same fire do is the only the business of those who share its tortillas."

"But Santiago will know about this, because I am going to tell him and everybody else is going to know about it too."

"The one who will say anything, if he wants to, will be Santiago," interrupted Me'el.

"What God damned story are you going to tell Santiago? It wasn't my fault that Antonio grabbed me that way. Why don't you beat him instead of me? If you tell Santiago anything, I am going to tell him to go screw up Antonio." Anita added with a breaking voice as she tried for the last time to defend herself.

"Lying kills," warned Me'el, "It hurts until death takes over, while the truth always ends up being understood."

Micaela did not answer. If don Antonio had waited for her there out in the woods, it was because he was used to seeing her there. But beyond that, right now, Me'el demanded peace and order with all of her resolve.

Anita assumed that she would no longer be seeing Antonio. From now on, every time she left their house, some of the children would be accompanying her. The little policemen would be watching over every visit and every cup of pozol that Ana took outside of the house and render their reports after every interrogation.

CHAPTER EIGHT

The May vacation arrived and Manuel unexpectedly showed up at the door. That was when Micaela realized how much time had passed by. She should have expected him because the corn was already planted. What a pleasure to see him. The days and hours to be with him were few.

Manuel breathed in the scent of his house. When he came in, he smelled the smoke and the patted earth he now walked on. He was no longer homesick because he felt at home. It smelled like beans. There was lots of racket and everyone's excitement made the gathering very emotional. Micaela said hello with the sign of the cross on his forehead and embraced him enthusiastically. Manuel went over to Me'el to receive her blessing too.

He noticed right away that grandmother was not moving around offering pozol to everybody, or serving up whatever there was in the house. Usually she would celebrate any visit not just Manuel's. She was always happy when there were visitors and Manuelito, who was special, had been welcomed as if he were a man ever since he was a small child. All because Manuel knew something, he spoke Spanish well.

Manuel asked about everyone, but there was no news about Santiago. The question seemed to cast a gloom over the gathering. He was relieved to learn that his older brothers wouldn't take long. They would come for their pozol later that night. Manuel had arrived at just the right time, because he would see them in a few hours. It was certainly going to be a cheerful gathering that night.

The corn was progressing well. Micaela told him that it had rained a little, those little showers that tend to loosen up the dirt. It seemed that there would be enough rain that summer, not like last summer. She and Me'el commented that it would be good for Manuel to take advantage of his vacation to work in the field. He shouldn't grow up without knowing how to manage a cornfield. In spite of the fact that no land would be his, he could count on his brothers' land and that way always have work and corn. Manuel wanted to go out to the cornfield, but even more, he looked forward to going out to the field the way he did when he was a child, when his father took him. He remembered that when he got tired, Santiago, trotting along like a little horse, would scoop him up into the air and put him on his shoulders. That way his transportation was assured, since Santiago never got tired.

He became excited and proud, as he thought about going. He enjoyed the hills and the contact with the soil, walking and working until he got all tired out and could not make another effort. Manuel wanted to spend some time with his brothers, his lifelong teachers, who had pestered him so much as a little child. For Manuel everything that Lorenzo and Sebastian did, was interesting. They were fearless and as far as he was concerned, experts on everything.

His sisters, on the other hand, were different not that they were afraid, they liked to run too, but Manuel found their fantasies boring and they spent too much time quiet and still. He played with them mainly to see their sweet faces because Mariana's smile was a jewel with its particular slant and lips that were dark and delicate but full. He always thought that her smile was the sweetest thing about her. She did not have to pretend to be a mother. So many years of carrying her little brothers around in her shawl had already left signs of maternal maturity in her. Manuel had been her first doll. He had been brought up in her arms and that is why he now recognized a source of protection in her warmth.

His arrival made everyone happy, even Anita, who had also cuddled him for many years. Domingo came over to get a good look, to be near him, and to touch him a little. Manuel was more than a brother for Domingo. He was the promise of security for his future, since Manuel would have to take care of Domingo when he went completely blind. For him, Manuel was an object of holy adoration, like a place sanctified by the Almighty.

Manuel accepted the role conferred upon him, superior felt superior even now that he felt so at home, their flatteries seemed normal. Tom with his sunburned hair and mischievous face moved over to him with a solemnity that was out of character for a brother.

"Good afternoon, Manuel," he said with a deep solemn voice, his head bent forward in front of Manuel, and quickly ran away.

"Tom, give me my hug," but little Tom flew away with a war hoop and Manuel had to chase him, running him down in the bushes to get his hug. He caught him and lifted him effortlessly up into the air, shaking him and letting him fall back with a suddenness that Tom loved. Manuel tickled him and tossed him up again. Tom not only played, he was everyone's favorite toy.

Curious about the uproar, Mariano arrived and so added joy to the occasion. Any friend of Santiago was always welcomed. Especially Mariano, because of the affection he bore for both Santiago and Micaela. He was like a brother to them. Micaela had not changed in all the time he had known them and Mariano remembered her well. He was the one who pointed her out to Santiago at the fair of the Candelaria, the second day of February already as prospects of the City Counsel, but couldn't be, since they weren't married so they would go down to the warmer low land to see beautiful women. She looked the same now as on that first occasion, with her shoulders bare, with a Tzeltal embroidery covering her body and the white lace that emerged from it accentuated the almost magenta tone of her dark brown skin.

Santiago made the first move and Micaela never turned him down. By the time their parents were aware of it, Mariano knew that it was already too late; Micaela was going to be Santiago's woman. Mariano looked for someone like her but never found her. He soon stopped looking. As it was, there were women enough in his home to do the work. With his older sister, widow with four children, his two younger sisters and his mother, all the chores got done. But despite living with all those women, Mariano still had no woman that loved him and him alone.

Micaela offered him pozol. Mariano had taken a lot of pozol in front of that fire, so he did not feel embarrassed by taking another one now and he sat down to chat with Micaela. They both needed a rest. Mariano filled her with optimism. He knew that Santiago's absence had to be aggravating simple household problems. He changed the conversation to talk about good things that had happened recently and good times ahead too. But the subject that most worried them kept creeping into their conversation and Mariano agreed with Micaela. Santiago should never have gone to the finca.

"Somehow, he could have found a few beans somewhere around here, but you have to keep in mind that if he left for money, it was for you, Micaela. You always need a bit to fix up the house, in order to tear down these adobe walls and put up a house with real material."

Mariano kept thinking that Santiago was probably the one who most wanted to be there, in his own home. Right now, he could have been sitting peacefully in his doorway keeping an eye on his little ones and watching Micaela. Mariano himself had great pleasure just by looking at her and listening to her even if he had no right to touch her.

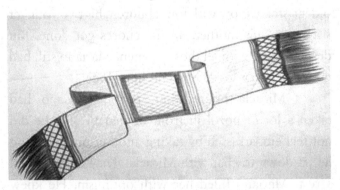

"Santiago won't be long in coming back, you know how much he enjoys being at home. If it is nice for anyone to be here, it has to be more special for him since he knows your ways, Micaela."

That comment slipped out inadvertently. He did not intend to make his admiration known to her, not because he was ashamed, but because he did not want to cause her any trouble. She was flattered by his glances. However much Mariano hid his desires, he was coming across to her as a man. She could not stop looking at him. He was atractive, his body was strong, still young, but his face had the scars peculiar to an interesting man, with bronzed skin and with callused hands. Watching him move, Micaela had no doubt of his manly qualities. She sensed an appealing smell, one given off by a body used to hard labor, not a predator or meat eating ladino's. Micaela felt now what she had not felt since Santiago's departure, an imperative growth of desire, which made her want what she had not wanted for a long time either, the weight of a man upon her. Micaela then realized that she had inadvertently ended up alone with Mariano inside the house and therefore she should not be there. The tenderness of his gaze was upsetting her.

Frightened, she stood up. She passed the edge of her rebozo over the place where she had been sitting when she was startled, to pick up any pieces of her soul that might have been lost. She courteously bade Mariano farewell with all the elegance of Tzeltal protocol.

Mariano went away as usual. He was used to Micaela dealing with him in a formal way. Through the years, he had lost hope of loving her, although over time Micaela had become even more interesting to him. He no longer thought in terms of the perfection of youth. He had learned to admire her through her children and Santiago just to keep her in sight. He kept in close contact with Santiago in order to keep on seeing her. After all, love flows like a great river, and the best of our intentions gets carried away by the current that disposes of our desires.

Mariano left the room, and despite herself, Micaela went over their conversation. She recalled every moment, each movement, and every bit of advice that they had offered one another. As she reconstructed the image of Mariano in her mind, that intense feeling that drives a person crazy, the most intense feeling there is in life, ran through her body again and she could not stop herself from liking it.

Micaela felt she had changed. Things that had seemed very clear were different all of a sudden. Every time she remembered Mariano, she felt the same thing. She spent the whole afternoon with his image around her. She knew she was doing wrong, but she continued nurturing her thoughts about him with every free moment.

That night with all of the children together in front of the fire, something that had not happened in a long time occurred, Micaela was not concentrating on the conversation. The older boys had come back from the cornfield for their pozol and found Manuel at home.

Enthused by the conversation and by the pox, they made plans to take Manuel back and teach him about their work. Manuel was excited. He wanted it to be dawn already so he could feel the fresh dew of their early departure. He wanted to be like his brothers, work like them and know that he was useful. Everything tasted delicious, especially after so much cold food at the students' home that always tasted the same, like nothing. Manuel knew that his birth place was a privileged one.

They got up before the sun did and the older boys led the way to the cornfield. They walked more slowly than usual because they knew that Manuel could not keep up the pace. At the boarding school he had become used to spending his time sitting down. They took care of vegetables there, but that was nothing like working in the field. Manuel did what he could to keep up with them.

On arriving at the cornfield after walking for two hours, Manuel was thrilled. That perfectly squared off section of land belonged to him too. All he had to do was stay there and cultivate it, and then no one would ever run him away. He let go of his sack and got ready. He wanted to begin to work with his brothers, but had a lot to learn first.

Sebastian took out the incense burner he carried in the net he knitted himself. He went over to the first corner and lit the resin. Smoke filled the corner, smoke that they thought would make more clouds, which in turn would bring more rain, so they all prayed. They prayed for good rain and that the rain still to come be better rain.

They prayed to the Saints and asked them to intervene, to protect their work and bring them water. They prayed similarly to the dead and to their grandparents that lived dead in the mountains. They left a little bit of food there for the Owner of the Earth, because, more than resentful, he was vindictive. They followed the path of sunlight then went north to protect that corner also, the same way, with the incense burner, with their prayers and with tricks in order to distract that accursed being. They protected each corner and then went to work. So no one expected a miracle, only the harvest they deserved from a year's work and that was the subject of their humble petition. They were confident that they were worthy of the fruits of their own labor.

From the moment the day began, Manuel felt the burden of the work on his back. His hands were getting stiff and his exertions made them burn. But gradually his body gave in and stretched out, and it looked like he was making good on his commitment. Manuel's hands were beginning to feel quick and agile. They attacked the weeds, pulling them out by the roots, as was necessary. He weeded for a while and then he began to break up the soil with his hoe. He kept on with his job until he felt like he was falling apart. He went back to the hoe several times during the day and lasted longer than his brothers expected. He stopped mid morning to wring the sweat out of his shirt. That was the only thing that added up to anything in all his life, the sweat in his shirt. Manuel took advantage of the rest period to eat a single lump of pozol.

He savored the dough slowly and then kept on working throughout the day as much as he could. When he looked to see how much progress he had made, he found that he had not covered an eighth of the ground that Sebastian had. And Lorenzo had done even more. It was better for Manuel to go off to one side, when he could no longer work.

He took out a second lump of pozol from his bag and seasoned it with chile and salt. He sat down to eat it and enjoy the view. When he had recovered resolve enough to keep on working, he went off into the woods in search of firewood. He gathered plenty for them to spend the night and he set the blaze going, all the while waiting for his brothers to give up and join him.

After a while they stopped working and came over to the fire to bid farewell to the end of the day. They tried to encourage Manuel by making up excuses for him, but instead of bringing him closer, they set him apart. The more they told him that he was young and inexperienced, the more they offered excuses for him to keep away from the work in the cornfield. At least that didn't keep them from being happy about being together working the land, besides, no one supposed that this would be Manuel's last try at being a man of the cornfield.

The lesson continued around the fire. The first course was the hardest, because they calmly talked about the dangers Manuel risked if he did not know how to take care of a cornfield. Whoever neglects his corn cannot expect a harvest. He ends up buying ladino food, even smelling like a ladino. He had to be careful, because betrayal comes little by little. The first steps occur unnoticed and then it seems normal to be a ladino. They didn't want to lose their brother. They depended on him and his studies. Most of all, they were concerned that his face and his body not take on a ladino shape, paunchy and overly delicate. They had to see that his hands had calluses, like a true farmer's and that he did not grow a beard or a mustache.

Lorenzo left to look for some bats to help Manuel. He found all they needed stuck to the soil in the dark hollows of the uneven ground. He managed to catch some by trapping them with his poncho and hat, then came back to the fire to prepare them. He mashed them up well and then stirred in some mud to make a paste that they smeared all over Manuel's face like a mask. That way, no beard would sprout and that at least made sure that Manuel could always come back to his homeland without looking like a foreigner among his own people.

Manuel slept peacefully that night. He slept deeply but he was so tired that, even after a deep sleep, he woke up tired in the morning. His muscles, rarely forced before to such extent, hurt. The muscles of his arms and lower legs hurt, and, above all, his hands burned. He opened up his fist and saw the dried blood. He had not noticed it there the night before, because the wounds were new then, and still warm.

He took a first step without warming up his muscles and felt painfully stiff. His grief and discomfort intensified. Manuel prayed for the day to pass quickly and for the sun not to punish him. He took up his hoe with great effort and in a slow, languid fashion began to dig in, while Lorenzo and Sebastian worked away, totally refreshed. They tried to encourage him.

"It's OK. You are just a little guy. You 're just not used to it."

Manuel was afraid of getting used to this. He did not want to spend another day like that nor weeks like that, much less a whole life time like that. It was hard and was too much to ask of him. The food at the boarding school was terrible and he suffered from cold and homesickness, but he never woke up feeling all beaten up. This pain served as a perfect excuse for him to avoid such annoyances in the future.

After sleeping five nights in the open, working from sun-up to sundown, and eating a few lumps of pozol, they returned home on foot. It was the same short walk, as before, just a two-hour walk, but those few hours seemed endless to Manuel. On the way back, he kept thinking and softened up whatever commitment his past made him have with his homeland. It was much easier to go back to school. That way, when his brothers needed him, he would be a respected person, able to help them.

Yes, life at the boarding school was easier, more comfortable, and less painful. But was there another type of man, a real man, like his father and the others who grew corn, who did not work the land? Manuel felt that he was drifting away from the only thing he knew about and loved without realizing that it was the summary of all the Mayan grandeur.

CHAPTER NINE

It was Mariano who decided to look for Micaela. He had been restless after their parting. When he arrived at her house, she was the first person he came across. Micaela was unable to disguise her pleasure at seeing him, for he still was her best friend.

She did not invite him in since she didn't want anyone to know he was there. She cut him off at once.

"I have to go for wood."

"I'll help you."

The proposal was simple, the temptation quite strong, that way she could talk with him without everyone else listening in on their conversation. Micaela took up her straps and discretely headed off toward the hill. No one saw her leave. She went without shame, as she was not one to be concerned about suspicions and intrigues. She had nothing to hide.

She was walking along with her usual graceful step. Mariano kept his eye on her and made her laugh. Instead of helping, he teased her by scattering the wood she had gathered. That was a game Micaela knew so she pretended to be angry. Enjoying herself, she flirted and Mariano egged her on so that he could hear her refreshing laugh after each scolding.

Micaela was the first one to get close. He could never have done it himself without her explicit permission, although he had often thought about it for many, many years. Now that the barrier was broken and they were no longer apart, he held her. There was no rejection. Micaela made it clear to him that she would go on even further. In any event, it was impossible to resist him. Having conceded a first kiss, she thereby consented to everything. She no longer hesitated, because she was concerned that any holding back could discourage him.

Mariano made no mention of how serious it was. He knew too much about life so he just kept quiet and held her tightly. It was too early to be sorry and too late to think about it anyway because her black hair was already tangled up among the dry leaves. With her clothes on, but her skirt lifted up and never taken off, only her belly exposed and her breasts uncovered as normally as her face was, Micaela felt Mariano's weathered but soft hands reaffirming their contact, pore by pore and curve by curve as Mariano's firm muscles and straight lines totally contrasted Micaela's figure which smoothly adjusted itself to his body and hands.

Their bodies danced there on the bed of pine needles to a rhythm set by pleasure itself, until fatigue took over and that was when a few drops of rain began to fall. They lay together for some time, waiting for the shower to let loose. The sun still shone, warming and illuminating the drops that fell, brilliant like crystals, and yet not enough to get them wet. Even the rain was as peaceful as they were and that gave them time enough to hold each other.

Mariano caressed Micaela's shoulders that showed through her low cut blouse. He was kissing her all over, and neither one wanted to leave. But time ran out and they had to part. The rain fell heavily and Mariano held her close for the last time, clearly letting her know that if there were any problems, he would take care of her. Micaela then realized that there was a chance she would suffer from now on. She felt her virtue exposed and out in the open and she began to cry from shame. Mariano held her tightly. He would not hurt her, and he comforted her, making her know that he understood her and that he knew that he had to go his own way, without counting on her.

And he did truly understand her despite the pain it caused him, but she came first, and he did not want to see Micaela suffer.

CHAPTER TEN

The sun appeared through a crack on the horizon. It tinged the sky with the brocade of a masterpiece on a handloom. A pink reflection came over the enlightened land. The dawn was decorated and all dressed up to welcome Santiago.

Tom, with his eagle eye, saw him first. The indistinct figure in the distance could have been no one else's. It was his silhouette, his walk and his manner. Tom recognized him from the hillcrest and, overjoyed at being the first one to see him, he let loose the cry of a warrior on guard and took off to greet him.

It was him. When Micaela finally realized it was true, she froze with joy. She had waited so long and the distant shape was unmistakably his. She wanted to run to him but couldn't. She was so overcome that she sat down and waited for the image she saw approaching to come close enough to touch it.

The joy spread around as fast as the news and soon other houses felt the contagious emotion. All the children ran over to Santiago and hemmed him in. In their enthusiasm they blocked his way. Tired and desperate, Santiago broke through and made one last effort to reach his house. His halting gait was not at all like his pace when he had left. The children crossed in front of him again and blocked Micaela's view. She could not see him well, so she didn't notice his fatigue, not his disorientation, or the overall deterioration of his body. Like a wounded soldier, he climbed up the last hill and took the tiny path that led straight to his door. It was his home, the one that he built and the one that he had kept warm for so long with his work.

Micaela was unable to speak even when she had him close by. Her weeping was interspersed with outbursts of nervous laughter that expressed nothing very clearly. She held Santiago tightly and then he let himself fall. Micaela did not understand what was happening and noticed he was trying to seek comfort on the floor. Before losing consciousness, he managed to ask them to take off his sandals, and he stayed there on the floor for a long time.

They immediately tried to waken him. They began to undo his sandals, but one of his hands stopped them and even pushed them away more forcefully than ever. He screamed and then was quiet, stretched out flat and breathing with extreme difficulty. Micaela saw the mud all over his feet and noted the blood mixed in with the dirt. Trying to loosen the straps, she saw the leather come loose with Santiago's flesh also. No wonder, he wanted them to take his sandals off, but didn't let them, his feet were as red as a blazing bath stone.

It was Me'el who thought of washing his feet first and loosening up the sandals with warm water. With patience and cold blood they took off his huaraches. They could not hurt him any more than what he was suffering already. He would get some relief from their care or at least the possibility of a little sleep.

There where he fell is where he slept and nobody tried to wake him up. Me'el and Anita continued with their housework but Micaela couldn't, and she sat by his side to watch over him while he slept. The children walked threw the room carefully in order to not wake him up. They could feel the tension, while Micaela spent hours sitting by his side without being able to take her eyes off of him. She wanted to see him now that she could, he was alive and she could not stop starring at him.

The sun set, the evening came, still Me'el and Micaela stayed seated at his side. Me'el suggested to her daughter- in- law that she lie down for a while, but it was useless. Exhausted as they were, they could not sleep. The spectacle of their man now decrepit, with his muscles all shriveled up, made it impossible.

Both women did not even blink as they stared at him. Santiago, the most stalwart among the councilmen, the man who made her feel like a woman just by looking at her, was now a great sorrow to behold. Micaela looked at this Santiago and remembered another. She could see his skeleton that was now noticeable beneath his skin and she grieved over the loss of flesh.

She trembled and wept when she saw Santiago in this state. She wanted to touch him but didn't dare. She let him sleep until he couldn't any longer and he didn't wake up until the afternoon of the following day.

When Santiago woke up, he felt like he had slept for only a few minutes, but if Micaela had told him that he had slept for an entire week, he would have believed her. He had no idea of the passage of time. He sat up with great difficulty and without a single complaint. He did not dare stand, so Micaela brought over a plate of beans. Bent over sharply on the dirt floor, Santiago didn't even raise the first spoonful of beans to his mouth. He was starving, but his hunger had passed the point of being felt in the stomach and had reached the point of deterioration that no longer lets you be aware of it.

He calmly took his tortilla, because he knew he had to eat. He soaked it in the bean broth and ate a little bit. Me'el brought over a cup of sweet pozol that was cool so it calmed him down. Then he lay down again. Micaela quietly just looked at him and stayed at his side. She waited for him to speak with the mature patience of a woman who knows how to wait for a harvest.

When he had enough strength to talk, Santiago asked about his cornfield. It was well under control, Micaela talked with him a little bit about it.

The elder boys had turned out to be good sons. Even Manuel had been introduced to the work. That was comforting to Santiago, as he had always thought that he had made a mistake when he sent Manuel to the boarding school. Santiago did not say another word. He ate slowly, taking a whole afternoon to finish off a dismal plate of beans. He did not ask about the other children, because they were all there, joyful and well, right in front of him.

That day he spoke as little as possible. He asked for another foot- bath with hot water and for a sack to lean his head on. Micaela asked no questions. She wanted to know what had happened to him but did not ask. She actually tried to avoid his having to remember it all. And she must have done right, because Santiago made absolutely no comments, not that day and not for many yet to come. Little by little, as Santiago began to drink, Micaela found out more things even though the more he drank, the less clear he talked and each day he drank more and more. The only words that could be clearly understood were the curses aimed at the patron.

CHAPTER ELEVEN

Santiago had always enjoyed sitting on the porch. He watched the sunset and so occupied the afternoon comfortably facing the countryside. He had a visitor. Don Miguel arrived to have a drink with Santiago, as he had done so many Sundays in the past. The five of them made themselves comfortable on the porch. Don Miguel brought the bottle as a gift and it passed from one hand to the next.

Miguel reported that things were going well for him. There had been some health problems at home, but otherwise everything was fine. At least, they had enough corn.

"We have enough to give you some, Micaela, if you need it."

"Thank you, compadre. You are very kind."

"In Chanal, they already obtained permits from the Forestry Department and it seems that the wood will be theirs. If they obtain it, we will get our permit too and will be less likely to run out of corn. That money won't solve all of our problems, but at least they will not be stealing our wood. The question for the people of Chanal now is just to negotiate well and as for ourselves, the government will have to hand over the permits to us. At least the woods are going to be taken better care of, cutting tree by tree and not the way those bastards chop them down, clearing off a whole mountain side at once. That way, someone else is not going to be taking off with what we don't use ourselves. I now believe that it was worthwhile to keep on struggling for so many years, what once belonged to us is finally going to be in our hands."

"It will certainly be different when you have the right to do the cutting yourselves. You are the ones who know the problem so you are the ones who can solve it. That way, you are going to take better care of the woods," said Me'el who knew that she was congratulating them on a great victory. "What isn't working out is the factory down there in Chilil. It doesn't get any orders and it can't get going."

"Business will pick up when they let us sell our wood ourselves, because as long as they have to buy wood from the big sawyers, they are only fattening up those outright thieves. But let's thank God that the new corn burst forth with so many flowers. You should have seen it this year, compadre. It looked like it had feathers of jade. The rain was lovely so let's see what surprise that might bring. The green spikes of corn are already dripping with sweet milk like a woman with a newborn baby."

Don Miguel always spoke that way. For him, each tree was like a hermitage and each sprig of corn, a sanctified cross. Clearly, Me'el no longer shared his optimism. Her innocent eyes had seen the woods disappear and she saw no way out of the situation.

"There are almost no woods left around here, don Miguel. If we have more wood here where the roads cross than in Oxchuc just think how thin the forest must be over there.

"How can there be more wood around here, Mother, if this soil is warmer?" said Santiago, who was annoyed.

There's no more forest around there, son, there isn't, even if you get upset with whatever I say." Since his return, Santiago easily got angry about anything at any time.

"Don't get upset, Santiago, the forest does look thinner. It's like the corn. There isn't enough any more. At least bananas grow around here, and cabbage and so many other things. We can get along just with the fruit. The pumpkins are beautiful and they're ready for the celebration of the dead." Micaela commented as she took the bottle of pox.

Alright, there are other things but if there aren't enough tortillas to eat, it's like there's nothing to eat.

"Nothing seems right to you, Santiago, but we must thank God that at least there is some fruit around," Micaela added.

To calm the discussion, don Miguel remarked upon how different the view was from his house, even though it was close by. It did not seem so to Santiago. Don Miguel, trying to be friendly, did want to include him in the conversation, but Santiago was not really listening to him. He just kept on drinking pox. He upended the bottle each time it went around.

"I went by your land, compadre. It flourished wonderfully, the cornfield looks quite even."

"At least there is some good news because that's all the money we have left."

Micaela had suspected that. If Santiago had arrived with money from the finca, he would have already brought it out. But the money was not as important as the fact that he was beaten up so badly. He was going to have to eat well now and they had finished off what had been left over from the sale of the little pig. Given Santiago's condition, he was not going to be able to work. He couldn't do anything except drink.

Micaela began to talk to don Miguel about Me'el's ankle. It was better but not yet fully recovered. Concerned about offering an opinion since it could upset the gathering he asked again how the fall had occured, above all because Santiago had not heard how it happened yet. Santiago listened, but being completely drunk, he did not hear. Don Miguel didn't like what he saw. Santiago was troubled, out of sorts and each time he lifted the bottle he began to scold Micaela.

"It was your fault," he told her. "You didn't take care of my mother." Micaela was frightened and began to cry. "Didn't I leave you in your home town? Didn't I leave you in your own house? Didn't I leave my mother in your care? Why do you put me to shame this way in front of my compadre? I left you with a garden. I left you with corn. You had no reason to leave home. You had no reason to leave and then have her fall down in Jovel. Could you ever have endured the hunger I put up with, ungrateful wretch?"

It was as if he had taken energy from the devil's breath. Suddenly he had enough strength to begin breaking everything. Micaela, just bewildered, stood up against the wall. She had never been afraid of him before, or had any reason to be afraid. Santiago usually became cheerful when he drank.

Me'el knew that he was not in his right mind. She exchanged glances with Micaela and knew that she was thinking the same thing. They looked at one another and knew that they had to be very careful not to say something that might bother Santiago even more, because anything could irritate him quite easily.

The children heard the uproar and came over thinking that dancing was about to begin. But when they saw Santiago take Miguel's machete out of its case, they only tried to protect themselves. Tom ran over to Micaela who tried to cover him with her shawl. In desperation, Santiago threw the machete at her. He was so drunk that the edge drove into the ground at his own feet. But Micaela did not escape his abuse he punished her with the palm of his hand. There was nothing she could do. Screaming or begging for mercy would only end up provoking Santiago. She had no idea what hurt more, her body or her pride, because between blows she could see that the children were watching it all.

Finally don Miguel dared to interfere. He never would have stepped in between a man and his woman, but Santiago was beginning to hit Tom now, who was desperately holding on to his mother.

"Quiet child, don't cry! I can't stand your screaming!" He shouted impatiently.

"Look Santiago, you're going to have to forgive me for butting into your affairs but If your father saw you now he would do the same thing for you. For your sake and in your father's name, may he rest in peace, I am going to put a stop to your crazy drunkenness."

Don Miguel did not think twice about it. He talked while he tied Santiago's hands to the posts in the doorway. It was not difficult to do, because Santiago did not put up any resistance. Don Miguel secured the ropes and stuck him up against the pole.

They left him there all night. At dawn, before he opened his eyes, Micaela untied his hands so he wouldn't soil himself out of anger. It was better that way, because Santiago didn't remember anything when he woke up. He lifted up his head and felt the pain. He felt that the dew had dampened his clothes. As uncomfortable as he was, he got up, complaining, irritable, and in a bad mood.

Micaela did not remind him of anything and Me'el had already put herself to making tortillas. They brought some over, taken right off the cooking pan, along with a few beans, his pozol and a little bit of dry chile. Santiago ate in penitence, without really knowing what his sin had been. He finished the meal without asking where it had come from. Having finished the plate, he handed it to Micaela with no sign of affection, not even a smile. Micaela would have pushed his arm away. She didn't want to be carressed by him smelling like that. She snatched the plate away instead of just taking it and left quickly to keep Santiago from seeing her look of anger. He would have noticed it. He would have noticed any look other than that of her usual humble smile.

While she poured water on the plate in order to rinse it she could not help remembering the beating. An intense ill will controlled the order the thoughts that were running through her mind. Not knowing what took her to it, she remembered Mariano. She recalled his courteous treatment and gentlemanly manners and she reconstructed the details of their encounter, each word, each touch, and his arms embracing her. The memory jarred her. She could not forget his image. It pleased her and she wanted it to happen again.

When Santiago needed her once more and called her, Micaela became aware of her distraction and she felt ashamed, the kind of shame that inhibits pleasure and destroys a home. She stopped working and stayed still. She was unable to go on with her work, or respond to Santiago's call. She saw that there were only a few beans left in the sack and she preferred to go out of the house without being noticed.

On other occasions when they had run out of beans, she was not that concerned, but now it only made the pressure worse. She wanted them to think she had gone out looking for pieces of pine to burn. She had no desire to look at Santiago straight in the eyes.

Santiago did not realize she was gone. His whole body hurt, and he could think of little else. He appreciated Anita bringing over a little coffee for him. He spent the whole afternoon beside the fire, with a lost look and without a word. He was not even aware that Micaela had returned and was rinsing off the dishes. There she was now, silent as usual, down on her knees on the dirt floor, next to Me'el. The grandmother broke in upon Micaela's wandering thoughts.

"Take it, Daughter, eat." She handed over the plate of beans and tortillas. "The only one who does not eat around here is you, Micaela."

"You need to eat too, Me'el."

Everyone has their share. I set aside a portion for the elder ones."

Micaela had forgotten that in a few hours the boys would be coming home. Beans were suddenly less appealing, because she wanted her sons to eat well. Me'el insisted, but it seemed that Micaela didn't want anything. She may have been hungry, but she had no apetite. Even though she had not broken her early mourning fast nothing seemed to appeal to her.

CHAPTER TWELVE

Lorenzo and Sebastian arrived earlier than usual. How they guessed is a mystery, but they always arrived when everyone missed them the most. Like a yoke of oxen, their steps went better together than apart. The house became cheerful as the boys filled it with noise. Santiago felt better with the joy of the afternoon. They were all so happy that a celebration was in order. At that point Santiago sent Anita out for a bottle of pox.

Anita came in looking for Me'el's bottle. She knew that Me'el had one, because she had seen Me'el take it out many times to ease her pain. Me'el refused to give it to her. She wanted to break it on the floor before Anita could find it, but Anita knew exactly where Me'el hid it. She searched and came across the aguardiente.*

"What's happening, Ana? Why are you taking so long?" Santiago shouted from the doorway.

"These women don't want to give it to me."

Me'el reluctantly handed over the bottle to Anita. There was not much left and that was when

---

* *aguardiente, liquor*

she realized that every day Santiago was getting more drunk with much less to drink. Anita thought she was still dealing with the same man she had known before. She had not been beaten, so it did not matter to her and she kept on doing his bidding. She took the bottle and went out to the doorway to celebrate Santiago's reunion with his boys.

As it was, with all the racket, the house was full of joy. Santiago loved just to be talking with his sons. They sharpened their machetes and talked about work in the cornfield. Lorenzo commented that it was growing beautifully and that Micaela's garden was also thriving, thanks to her care. They could count on her effort this year also.

They took Sebastian's knife and played by throwing it and making it land inside a circle marked on the ground. They were together and happy, Manuel, Domingo, and even little Tom, filthy as always for no matter how often they washed him, he was always dirty. He too played with his father, throwing the knife, and on his first turn, he hit the center of the circle. He celebrated his good aim loudly enough to make himself hoarse. Now it was Lorenzo's turn. Leaving his own sharpened machete on the floor, Lorenzo threw the knife. It landed on one side of Tom's good throw. Lorenzo stepped aside to wait for another turn. While waiting, he wanted to keep on sharpening the machetes, and he asked Santiago for his, so he could give it a new edge.

"Give me your machete, father, I will sharpen it for you while you play."

Santiago lowered his head without answering. He did not move, apparently thinking and then he began to cry. Lorenzo was sorry because that is when they all realized that Santiago had returned without his machete.

The bottle passed from hand to hand, from Sebastian, to Lorenzo, to Manuel, but it always ended up in Santiago's hands. They took tiny sips because there was not much left. Only Santiago turned the bottle upside down until he finally finished it up.

He started to demand another bottle. Me'el was glad not to have one and Micaela was not too concerned because she no longer had enough money for another. But Anita was enjoying herself, especially now that Santiago was beginning to play with her breasts and her braids. She gave money to Tom and sent him out for another bottle. Micaela saw her hand out the precious pennies that they needed every day at home.

"Your money is going to harm you."

"Whatever will harm me will be what you will be thriving for," answered Anita. Micaela, not even pretending to disguise her anger, pulled at Anita's hair. It was not enough to hurt her, but Anita cried out at the top of her voice. Santiago came in limping to check on things and Anita immediately accused Micaela.

"Did you really hurt her? You not only neglect my mother but you also abuse my unborn child!"

Micaela, of course, had forgotten that Anita was expecting a baby when she pulled her hair. It was past time for explanations, because Santiago decided to inflict swift justice. She began to feel the weight of his arm as he beat her. Anita intervened, asking Santiago that he not pay attention to that wretched woman.

Micaela went over to a corner to cry. Again the children had seen it all, even Manuel and the older ones. Aparently Manuel was affected the most because an insurmountable animosity toward his father began to grow within him.

His aggression was as unexplainable as all his other reactions so Manuel felt sorry for his mother and felt more close to her now than ever. He understood her, because he knew how long she had waited for his father. He had already seen her suffer too much. She was the one he missed the most at the cold boarding school. He wanted to comfort her, but Micaela pushed him away, since each of Santiago's reactions seemed to make less and less sense.

Manuel moved off to one side not knowing how to help, and Santiago ordered him out and to leave that wretch where she was. Santiago was hardly able to stand upright but went over to the door again to find out about the other bottle of pox. Tom had not yet returned with it and Santiago was in a hurry.

"Send the other child out for another bottle. Whatever little Tom brings can be left for another occasion."

Micaela could not believe it. Anita had money for another bottle. Santiago never asked where the savings that seemed inexhaustible for the pox, came from. How could he not realize what was going on? Micaela was tempted to tell him but suddenly realized she could not say anything. She understood clearly that evil was falling upon the house because of so much sin.

Little Tom arrived with the other bottle of pox. Santiago insisted that they drink it with him and he finished more than half the pint of pox himself. When Micaela first met him, he would have been able to finish off an entire bottle and keep on going till the party ended, but now it looked like he was going to end the party instead. And it did end promptly, when Santiago began to insult all of them.

Poor Manuel, Santiago hit him in cold blood for having embraced his mother. Where did he get the strength? He had taken on another face, another expression, another color. He had turned yellow. Perhaps that was the evil that don Miguel mentioned when he saw him go crazy, an evil that turns people yellow, and by then, there's nothing you can do.

It was just as well that Mariano arrived. Don Miguel had already told him that ever since Santiago's return, he did not seem to be in his right mind. Mariano went over and embraced him. He held Santiago tightly and let him cry. How carefully Mariano took control of Santiago. He was still his best friend.

"Look brother, you don't know what you do when you are drunk. Something rotten comes out of you and you need to get it out of your heart. Sit down and tell me what's wrong so you can get this sadness out of your soul. Otherwise that bitterness is going to hide there and will reappear when you least expect it to."

Mariano was preparing the ground for expiation. With Micaela crying at his side and his mother testifying to everything that had happened, Santiago finally took heart and began to talk. Only the moon kept track of the time. Mariano didn't, he had all the time that Santiago could need in order to start letting out what was bothering him. From that moment on, Me'el relaxed because she saw that Santiago's look had regained its own sparkle. It was his first open dialogue with his soul. He began to let loose, the catharsis had begun, as he started to tell them all he had suffered at the finca.

CHAPTER THIRTEEN

"You probably won't believe me but I can still remember what I felt when I first set foot on the soil of the finca. We walked for five whole days before we came face to face with the boss. The coffee harvest began that very same day. The bushes were covered with beans. We wanted them to pay us for each can we picked. It's better for us that way since we can fill up a sack quickly. But no, that's not the way the patrón*

---

* patrón, owner of the plantation or boss

saw things. He just stood there to make sure we would make the best of each morning and work without stopping. Afterwards, as the beans grew scarce and they had almost finished, he began to pay by the can, but by that time it took several hours to fill one up. That was how sly the lousy patron was."

"So, when I first arrived at the plantation, they gave me my place in the sleeping shed. You know, brother, how the fincas are. There is one side for us and over there, on the other side, lived the patron in that big house of his. Wow, that house had alot of rooms, with big, long hallways but always empty, because the boss lived alone with fear and no woman, well no woman you would call his. They said that he had a wife, or had had one, and that she charged him a lot in order to raise his children far away from there. The fact is that I never saw that house full. It was just for him alone."

"Not even the armed guards lived there. They lived separately from us too, for no reason other than that they were also bastards. They were poor like us but didn't like poor people. They defended the patron, but did not like him either. They always had nicer houses; not like the patrón's, and didn't eat like the patrón either. They were just a little less poor than we were, that's all, but their hearts were already a little rotten like the boess's."

"Well, as it happened, I made a friend who had been born there on the plantation, don Gabriel,

who was very good to me. He gave me a little bit of room in his house and I helped him, because the boss gave us some cooked beans and half a kilo of tortillas to each of the workers, but didn't give anything to don Gabriel because he had been born there so he was assigned a corn patch of his own. Ever since he could remember the boss lent him a little piece of land to raise a few sacks of corn for his family to eat. He had no tools and no seeds, just a wretched little piece of dirt so he could make their own food, as though my compadre ate dirt! He had to do everything by himself from planting the corn to making the tortilla just so he could eat because on top of taking care of his own piece of land there was the Patron's cornfield to attend without pay all in exchange for the small piece of land he lent my compadre for him to grow his few sacks of corn. He had to pick coffee for almost no pay and work the patron's cornfield without pay. That was not all the patron wanted. Don Gabriel had to pass on gifts to the lousy patron to keep him from getting pissed off."

"We got tired of hearing the boss say he didn't like any kind of lack of respect or that we weren't paying enough attention to him. And four abused housemaids waited on the patron, just for him to be well dressed. The day began at the same time for them as for us, because the patron never ate reheated left over tortillas. As soon as the sun showed its face, that was the hour for us to start bending over, or so the patrón said."

"Sundays were not paid, but that didn't make any difference. We had to work in the patron's cornfield and then I helped my compadre with his. On Sundays, which was payday, I also had to carry water up to the big house. It was near the river, in a better place, but it was just as hard, because the big house used a lot of water."

"And my compadre always lived more than five hundred yards back from the river. It took a lot to carry water there and how the women struggled to carry enough over, since they didn't have someone to fetch it for them. That's why we always needed to help the women. Whenever I had a chance to rest I would bring them some wood or look after one of their little ones for a while. Even worse when something ailed them, because who knows why there's always something bothering women, the fact is that they can put up with more problems than we can, but in the meantime, they're always complaining."

"And there is always sickness. My friend's children had huge sores on their faces and ulcers all over their bodies that they couldn't get rid of, no matter what they did. It was a stubborn ulcer that

 settled on the skin and my comadre Tina tried to cure it with the saliva of a toad. I don't know what hit me each time I saw the treatment. The toads were what disgusted me and even more so with the way they stink when they bust out that white slobber."

"Poor little kids, there was just no way to make them get well. Anyhow, at least I didn't have that problem. Only worse things happened to me. I spent my time with my compadre. In the evenings people got together at his house. There was always a racket no shortage of talk and even dancing. It got worse when the Pentecostals or what ever their name was, showed up. You know how they say to forget this world and just think about the one that is coming. My compadre and I saw things differently. We were in a hurry to see our people live better lives. Those Pentecostals said justice would come with death. But my compadre said little children need their food when they are still alive, not afterwards. Afterwards, what for?"

"And my compadre certainly had enough little ones including one darling young girl who had not seen over fifteen harvests. She kept staring at me with the eyes of a little woman, but I didn't take her up on anything instead I enjoyed her company. She was my friend's little treasure. No Gabriel's little girl was not something that you could just take for a ride and forget. I would have had to take her with me but I couldn't take care of her. I wasn't the only one who would stare at her, they all did. And when they got ready to dance, they put the young girl in the center so she would walk there all alone and everyone could stare at her. As for myself, I made it seem I was unaware of her glances. We became companions. Wherever I went, I took her along with me. I would even take her to the river, can you imagine that, I used to take her along to swim in the river. The cutest nooks of her skin turned pink from the sun burn. Just imagine how hot I got seeing her soaking wet afterwards."

"When the discussions began, there was the girl, just listening and paying close attention. The discussions were long. Sometimes all night long. The patron did not let us get together so we had to get up early in the morning or wait for the armed guards watching over us to get drunk. My compadre always began the discussion, especially when the Bible people, the shouters, visited him. They prayed by singing, but my compadre spoke frankly to them. Forget about death, he told them and join the struggle. My friend was very brave and that was why the patron did not like him, not a bit. That way, little by little, I learned what organization was all about. In the beginning I did not understand it, because that word is so long and difficult. My compadre would say that the only way I would understand it was by going step by step, because we are like ants, and we must learn which leaves from the highest branch of the greenest tree are the sweetest but no one is going to believe us if we tell them. We have to pass by them with those leaves in our hands and when they see us go by with the leaves and ask us where we got them from, we only have to show them the way so that they can find them by themselves. We never want to lead them by the hand. Little by little we will become many and then we may become strong, because no one was taken, we all found them by ourselves. That way we will reach an agreement, because that is what Organization is, it means all of us reaching an agreement."

"At times it was difficult for me to understand the things my compadre said, but I learned. My compadre taught me alot of things! One day some Guatemalan refugees came all the way over the line to where we were and it was don Gabriel who helped them, he was that good. The corn was not ripe, but we gave them the early ears to eat. We even killed baby turkeys, made some elegant soup, and fixed up a cozier corner of the hut for them, by piling up some sacks just to give them a little bit of privacy. They had nothing, because all they owned had been burned up. They told us that in their homeland, they were killing all the poor people. They just couldn't understand why all of this was going on. But the Guatemalans said that that was why they had to flee. Now, there were no workers left to build their big houses or peasants left to work on their great plantations.

"They had all lived in Cuarto Pueblo, where, on the 14th of March, at eleven in the morning, the army came in and suddenly surrounded them. It was Sunday and the market was full. When the people saw themselves being rounded up, a few tried to run away, and that was when the shooting began. After that, no one got away, and they were held together the whole day Sunday. They held all of them Monday, Tuesday, and it was on Wednesday that they set them on fire. They burned some of them up in the Evangelical Chapel, others in the kitchens of the plantation and in the clinic, and more of them in an old school. And that was what happened on that Wednesday. Then they grabbed ten cattle from the pasture, about a hundred quintals* of cardamom* and even more quintals of coffee, and they took off with all of it in some helicopters in the direction of a place they said is called Playa Grande. Since these Guatemalans fell down wounded when the shooting first started, they pretended to be dead and managed to see it all."

"By now there was nothing left for them but to take their smallest child with them thinking they were going to take him to his holy burial but the little child was alive. He just looked dead, he was that

---

quintals* 100 lb. bale and cardamom* a plant of the ginger family

quiet, but he was alive, and with God's blessing, he began to cry just as they crossed over the border. It was a blessing also that the child did not cry on the way out because the ones that cried had their mothers cover their mouths so tightly that they passed away in their mother's arms. These poor people came all the way over to the finca where I was. I have never seen anyone so poor even though I have only seen poor people all of my life. They said that there were many of them, only that most of them stayed back along the border, just on this side of the line. Many of them now had no children left. No bullets were wasted on children. The soldiers simply threw them down onto the rocks. How painful for their mothers, who had to see the heads of their children bashed in! Now in their own land, back there, all that remains are piles of bones, little bones of little people, and big bones of great people."

"It was best for them to stay away from the border, and avoid being forced to go back under any circumstance. They could not understand why this was happening. All they knew was that the government had never paid any attention to them. They paid a tax, everyone had a tax certificate, but the soldiers still came in all enraged and killed them. Don Gabriel enabled us to see things clearly, because he was the first one to help them. They were just like us, of our kind and that's why he had to help them. It was for the best that we protected our Guatemalan brother and took him along with us wherever we might go so that he might forget things. As you know brother, there are some sorrows that take a lot of work in order to be forgotten."

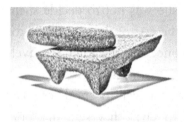

"Boy, they were good at cultivating vegetables and weeding! They were real dynamos with the vegetables, never missed a single worm hidden under any cabbage. We kept a close watch on them so they could forget their grief. When Holy week came along we celebrated it together since we prayed to the same Saints as they did. They cheered up. It was then, right in the middle of dancing, that my comadre Tina began talking about how expensive everything was, especially at the boss's store. Tina said that her bill there just couldn't be paid for. She paid and then paid a little more and there was no end to it. So that's how I fell right into the middle of the struggle, because they commissioned me, they gave me my assignment."

"The following day, instead of helping my compadre in his cornfield they sent me with everybody's money to buy bedclothes, oil and even a hand mill for my comadre Tina, who wanted ever so much to be able to straighten up her back while she ground the corn. Then my compadre's child invited herself to go along with me, because she had not even been to Niquivil and wanted to at least visit Motozintla some day. She wanted to travel and see places. There was nothing between us so I knew it was fine for me to take her, but her father scolded her and clearly told her that she was not to decide such things all by herself, that the rest of the group had to agree. Otherwise, what money was she going to travel with?"

"I learned that way never to speak of "I." From then on I learned to say: "they sent me," or "we decided," or "we want," or "we think." But as the racket went on all night and we made the girl walk around so we could look at her, everything got quite cheerful. And after a lot of drinking and a lot of pleading from the child, her father gave her permission to help me with the load of bundles. Since this was the first time she'd left home, she couldn't care less about coming back loaded down with heavy bundles."

"The young girl took off happily that morning. I offered her tamale with beans and I saw how she acted more like a woman."

"She was happy and since I am a gentleman I treated her like a lady, and, since there was nothing between us, I took her casually through the streets she tried so hard to memorize. We went on to the Bureau of Land Reform just as my compadre had asked me to and that was the beginning of my downfall, because on the way out, I ran right into the patron, who was leaving, just after having had a drink near by."

Chapter XIII

"I thought he would not know who I was, but as I was passing him, he saw the young girl and recognized her. Indeed, how would he not know her, because he already had it in his mind to do her harm? He knew her well. Several times now, he had demanded her from my compadre. And my compadre didn't say anything, but we all knew that only over don Gabriel's dead body could he harm his precious little virgin. The guy was leaving the place and that was how he became familiar with my face."

" "Where are you going, chamulita?" he said to me."

"And I told him that I was from Oxchuc, not from San Juan."

" "Now who are you to talk back to me like that," he replied, "let's see what you have there. What makes you think you are going to do business with my Indians? You'd better be careful!" That was all he said, with his customary snakelike face and belly all set to explode."

"It's not business, sir," I answered. "It's only because we find better prices here. I was doing the others a favor by doing an errand for them."

"He gave me a scorching look, grabbed his truck, and took off in the direction of the plantation. We were left there, the child and I, with our fears and our purchases and he took off in his empty truck, just for himself. I took one look at the young girl's face and I forgot about the lousy patron. I bought her a big lump of gum and we went on our way along the little path, happy enough. When I reached the finca there was my surprise because the authorities were waiting for me."

"Where are you coming from, bastard?" I think that was his greeting."

"I went on an errand," I answered, since it was true."

"And what did you buy?"

"A blanket."

"A blanket or blankets? You sure have enough there. You stole them, right? Where are the receipts? Where did you get money to pay for things like that? You stole that too, didn't you?"

"This guy must have helped the other one steal the cow. They are always together."

"And so, I came to understand that the big complaint was with my compadre, but they did not dare to mess with him, because we were many and quite ready to give up our lives for him. I think that was why they began to give me a hard time. They knew how much it would hurt my compadre and that very few of them around there knew me enough to defend me. It would have been better if they had tried to mess around with don Gabriel, because then, they would never have been able to do anything. We would have realized in time what they were going to do and all of us would have stepped forward to protect him."

" "Let's see the receipts" added the one who had greeted me so elegantly."

"What do you mean?"

"Keep on pretending your innocent, idiot! Where are the receipts?"

" "I don't know what those things are." He didn't want to believe me. He only believed the boss when he lied to him."

"I tell you that this is the one that helps him steal cows. I may not have actually seen that old guy, but this one I have seen."

"Are you sure that you saw him, yourself?"

"I sure did. I saw him."

"Then inside you go, bastard. That's where the money must have come from for your business with the bedclothes."

"He had to push away my compadre, who by that time was at my side, defending me. My compadre should never have done it, because from then on the patron never left him in peace."

"This one is always getting into things that are none of his business. Let's teach him right now what can happen to him. You are going to end up like this little friend of yours who does errands, because men don't do errands. We are going to make a man out of him."

"The fact is that they tied me up with tight ropes cutting into my arms and then they put me into a little box, the one they use for punishment, according to the lousy patron. Dona Tina was the only one who had permission to come over to that cage when she brought the five tortillas the boss allowed me to have, along with the bottle of liquor too, but not fine nich*, no, that cheap stuff, the one that makes your head swell up. If I did not finish my drink, they were not allowed to bring any more tortillas to me. That was to keep me cheerful, said the patron, spirits to keep my spirit up."

"There I was, hanging on from one visit to another, and one day I asked my comadre about the young girl. I wanted to find out if the vicious patron had taken revenge on her too. Doña Tina was not allowed to spend much time with me, so she told me briefly that every day the patron made her thank him for having left the child alone, even though she too had broken the law, he said. If she were loaned to him a few nights, he would see that the charges brought against her were lifted."

"My comadre, out of pure fear, kept her little daughter well hidden. But when the patron was drinking, he would yell out and demand: "Ungrateful Indian! Bring over the girl.""

"And my compadre seethed with rage. It must of been very hard on my Comadre because just mentioning it made her cry. It would have been better for her not to say anything, since I couldn't help her any way. The armed guard was listening in, so I was only making things worse for her by giving her more problems."

" "You know that you can't talk to someone who is punished," he told her."

"I tried to speak out strongly in her defense. "I didn't know. I was the one speaking," I told him."

"Look, you bastard, if you ever get out of here, I think it'll be better if you leave all messed up. Bastards like you always cause problems when they get out."

"And that was when he did this job on my feet with a sheath knife. When he took it out of his pocket I saw the glimmer of its sharp edge. That was the brightest light I saw the whole time I was inside there. I did not count the rising suns, because their beams never struck my face. The point is he tied my sandals back on with my feet all smeared up with manure. That was how I got these sores because I had to pee on myself, do everything all over me and the urine drained down stinging me through my pants and burning my flesh."

"It was only through that hole in the wall that a little hope came in when my comadre arrived with tortillas, no salt, and with the drink they made her give me. She would put it in my mouth and whisper softly, "We are not going to let you die, compadre. We are not going to let you die.""

"That was the way that I found out that they were taking legal steps to get me out. My compadre did not sleep just thinking about what I was going through, but the legal process was very complicated. They needed more documents and my compadre did not know how to read or write. My comadre said that it was hard to get me out, because the patron wanted me to serve as an example, so that the rest of them might know what could happen to them if they went around trying to become his equals also."

"Who knows how I got out, but one day I did get out and the punishment was over. The first thing I did was wash myself in the river with a little soap that my comadre Tina gave me. I took off the sandals, the rotten clothes and tried to sleep a little, but not for very long, because soon, shortly after, one of the gunmen showed up."

" "We don't like lazy bastards around here," he said."

"And he took me out into the shrubs to work. He watched me all day long, making sure that I did not speak with anyone, or stop working. I believe that I never got my strength back and never was able to stop drinking. My comadre was rationing it, so I would gradually drink less, taking small portions at a time, because it was impossible to take it away from me all at once. What was worse, I had to work straight through, hungry, with the sun overhead and spiders all over me."

"I didn't sleep not even at night, since they did not let me sleep in my compadre's house anymore.

I was going to abuse the young girl, according to the patron and then he wouldn't have her virgin. Of course, I was not going to do anything to that girl, the dear treasure of my friend because I loved her the way one loves anything that is good and full of life. The little girl had become so silent. My compadre said that his daughter no longer danced and that her laughter, that used to be as cheerful as a waterfall, was gone."

"That was when we realized that we could no longer stay at that accursed finca but the problem now was that there was no way to leave. My compadre was well on his feet, but not me, I could not even manage to walk a league."

"You will make it," said my compadre. "If you can survive this awful work, you can make it back home."

"That's when we all decide to leave together besides my compadre was tired of going to Tuxtla to find out what had happened with his land rights. That was the only reason why he wanted to stay because he could leave my comadre at my house and I guess that was what he wanted to do, to get her out of there along with the little newborn that I baptized myself. He would bring them here to Cuxuljá and then go back to truely fight for his land."

" "They are going to kill you, compadre," I told him."

"True," he answered, "but we were born to die and it can't be anything worse than dying."

"Then I understood him. Now, with his wife safe, he could struggle on with no distractions. But how was my comadre going to accept an arrangement like that if she was part of the struggle too?"

"No, husband," she said. "You go. Take the girl to Santiago's house. I'm going to stay here to take care of our stuff. What happened to the Guatemalan can happen to us and they can take everything we have away from us."

"My comadre was that strong but thank God, she stayed at her house, while we were stupid enough to think we would get away from the patron. Anyhow, we were happy when we started out in the middle of the night. Don Gabriel's daughter went on ahead. She did not know that we were watching her so she skipped along with nimble little steps, moving gracefully along the path. I thought that my face had lost whatever appeals to women, but her eyes told me that she still liked my style."

"That must have been the last time she liked a man's ways, because at that moment the Guatemalan shouted out."

"Careful, there are some bastards moving around over there."

"And, yes, they were bastards. They said so themselves, the first thing they said was that they were from the government. We kept still, because as soon as we saw the look in their eyes, we knew they were bastards. Poor Guatemalan! Why did he even dare try to find better luck? Right away they asked him about his boots. And us, we never noticed that he wore different shoes. He was just like us, our race, just our kind of people. We hadn't even looked at what he wore on his feet."

"He was the first one they screwed. One of them came up and said he was from the Migration Service and that no refugees were allowed there. They said he was illegal and just for that they took away the few pennies he carried and then they really worked him over. How ashamed I was that such a thing could happen to the Guatemalan in my own country. Perhaps he was better off, because right then they took him away, not without taking the few rags we had found with great effort for him to wear. They took him away with just his underpants on and without telling his wife. He kept quiet since he was afraid they would come in after her and take her away also."

"They swore they would not kill him. They were going to take him back to his own land now. The killing seemed to have stopped because there was no one left to kill. He said that on the other side of the border they were locking up poor people in some big pens where you cannot even keep a hen of your own and you live the whole time under the watchful eyes of the authorities."

"I wanted to take off for the mountain, but they threw a rope around my hands and tied me up under a tree. They were going to beat me up, they told me, for going off and trying to escape. After filling my mouth with dirt and manure, they covered it up so my lips could not move. They did the same to my compadre. They tied us there so we could see everything. That was when the patron showed up."

" "Yes! That's the one," he said, pointing to my compadre. "That's the one that just plain doesn't want to stay still. He goes around stirring up all the Indians and this is the little girl he doesn't let grow up. I have told him many times I'll take care of her." "

"The poor little thing, I could feel her shaking from where I was. They hurt her and they laughed. The more it hurt her the more they would do it. How they hurt her and it wasn't even possible that they could be enjoying it and they laughed, and did not stop until she, now a woman lost consciousness. My compadre closed his eyes. Then I realized that my compadre would not live to see another day, because the patron knew that after this, he was going to have to kill him. Either my compadre died or the patron did. That is why they put him inside that sack and I only saw blood come out of that sack. Who knows how the gag fell out of his mouth, but from then on, we heard his screams. And my compadre wouldn't die. My compadre wouldn't die! I only asked God to take him up to His sacred side."

"They said that now it was my turn, and, by the way they spoke I noticed that they were not from around here. They spoke real fast, sort of singing, not a bit like we speak. And I thought that I too was going to be another dead one. But no, with me they were just having fun."

" "Look! His paws are already getting better," said the patron who seemed to know what it meant to screw up a man's foot if he depends on his footsteps. They calmly smoked a few cigarettes and put them out on my wounds." "

" "Put his shoes on tight," said the patron. "So he doesn't get hurt on his way home and blame it on us." "

"That was how I found out I was going to end up alive, since I was at their mercy, and depended on whatever they decided, and I did live, because then the boss said:"

"Let this one go so he tells the other Indians back home that around here the boss's law is backed up by the government."

"And the last thing I thought was that if this is government, then what the hell do we want a government for?"

"From that point on I was aware of nothing else. What with all the beatings, I lost consciousness. When I woke up I was someplace else. Who knows how long I spent at the bottom of that gully? I could not loosen up my sandals. Following the sun through the mountains, I arrived home. Who knows if my compadre is in heaven, who knows if the young girl will ever smile again and who knows why God allows a hell like the fincas."

CHAPTER FOURTEEN

The older boys went back to the cornfield. They preferred being out in the open than to stay and watch what was happening at home. Me'el hobbled off to prepare their pozol for the road. They said good-by to their grandmother and Micaela, but not to Santiago, because he was still asleep.

"Who am I?" Santiago asked when he woke up crying.

Micaela could not help herself from being on his side. She felt him holding on to her tightly and begging her to help him.

"We are going to be ourselves again. These are wounds that only time knows how to cure. We must let the sun take its course and let it bring us a new day, take us to new dawns, each one brighter, each one more brilliant and you will see our trials forgotten some new day when a new sun surprises us with a bright unknown glare."

Micaela was crying too and now she was unable to help Manuel get his things ready to go back to the boarding school. It was Me'el who helped him. She gathered up his clothes, put pozol in his

ᘒᘒᘒᘒᘒᘒᘒᘒᘒᘒᘒᘒᘒᘒᘒᘒᘒᘒᘒᘒᘒᘒᘒᘒᘒᘒᘒᘒᘒᘒᘒᘒᘒᘒᘒᘒ

knapsack, a little chile in his bandanna and then embraced him.

"Young man, you've seen things that you shouldn't have at your age, but never judge your father for what we have to suffer. Don't forget us. Only here will you find people of your own blood and you will be in danger if the distance grows between our home and the path you are following. Be careful and may your heart never become as cold as the hallways of that boarding school."

His grandmother's advice frightened Manuel. He swore never to forget his home, or his people. But he did leave. He bade farewell to his parents and did not come back home for over seven years.

Santiago played with the little baby that Anita had given him. He was walking now and saying his first words. Anita's belly slowed her down. Soon she was going to be giving birth again and would need help, but Me'el no longer had strength enough to help her. Micaela and the girls did everything. They carried the water, built up the cooking fire and without anybody telling her to, María Rosa began to sprinkle water to fill the room up with steam. Once the steam bath was fired up, Micaela began to give advice to Anita so she would stay calm. Anita missed Me'el's wisdom, but the grandmother could not even get close to her.

Santiago, with his feet still affected by his injuries, drew near just to hold her hand.

"Don't be afraid woman. It will be born the same way the first one was," he said.

All the while, Micaela and the two girls kept on working. They knew exactly how babies came into the world and they knew that it was just as hard every time.

Domingo and Tom kept away from the house. Their heads down, they headed off for the hillside, with no idea of what to play at. Domingo, whose eyes were almost useless now, needed help to keep from stumbling. Tom showed him the way. They were heading toward the river, because that was the best place to head for. Me'el wanted to catch up with them.

"Don't go far," she shouted.

She went off after them, walking in spite of her pain. She took one step and then another and began to walk without fear, because all of a sudden the pain was going away. She took each step eagerly, and now the pain was gone. Her face was gladdened and she began to laugh. She trotted along with the gait that had served her all her life and there was no pain. That was when she realized that each step she took went from the summit of one mountain to the summit of another and that she could see it all, everything. Through the shingles and the strips on the roofs, she could count the people, the people of today and the people of yesterday, the grandparents, her parents, her Aunt Lucia, always sick, and her brother Alonso without work. She could see everything there was to see in all the houses, in each wagon, and in every corral. She was thinking about everything that needed to be done, the births, the curing of the sick, the celebrations, and she calculated. She calculated the way so many, many years of practice had taught her to. She calculated that nowhere would it allow waiting for the corn to be picked, and then, after that, they would have to squeeze out even more, one tortilla less for each child, one day less of beans per week, while there, off in the distance, the sardonic laugh of a ladino sounded.

But little lights were going on here and there. They were multiplying and they were confusing to her. More laughing was bursting forth from the children and from joy itself. And by walking along that way, from the top of one mountain to the top of another mountain, hill by hill, temple by temple, she arrived at her destiny. On leaving her land, Me'el understood that not even now had a glimmer of hope emerged out of the long anguish of her people, a people defeated long ago and still subjugated. Finally, with no ilusion of hope, she joined the glory of her ancestors.

Dr. Thomas Whitney's note

The following words appearing in the text are not translated. The following are suggestions as to the meaning of these words and expressions.

Aguardiente – liquor or spirit of distilled sugar, common but clandestine in Chiapas

Chapincito – **Chapin refers to a type of footwear. Chapincito is used in Central America in** reference to Guatemalans of indigenous origin and is translated here as "the Guatemalan."

Comadre and compadre – literally, godmother or godfather, person who holds a child during his baptism so it usually refers to a special adult, longtime friend, often one with a mentoring role.

Finca – a plantation, a farm of unspecified size, one that in Southern Mexico produces crops such as sugar, coffee, bananas or cacao and that requires a large amount of hand labor, often provided by migrant workers.

Ladino – Among the word's several meanings, there are two that are relevant here: one, a person of mixed or full Hispanic heritage, i.e. less than pure Indian, and, two, a person who is crafty or sly. Indigenous people in Central America and Mexico often apply both meanings to a single person. The term refers to a tricky person and definitely not pure Indian.

Nahuales – An animal soul present when a child is born. It may depart later on, during times of trouble.

Pox – an alcoholic drink of distilled sugar made in the home with primitive fermentation methods. The same as aguardiente explained above,

Pozol – corn made flour and moistened enough to allow it to be carried as a lump.